ANNA'S EYES

Her eyes were closed; she might have been asleep. Travis thought again how delicate she was. Without conscious volition he moved to the side of her, put his hands, gently, on her shoulders. It was the first time he had touched her. Even this trivial intimacy was shockingly intense. Her skin was cool; it was as if he could feel her fragility under his fingers. She stirred but did not open her eyes.

It was strong, he thought, this thing that was special about her—stronger the closer he got to her. . . . He stroked her perfect cheek, and she trembled.

"Anna?"

Her eyes were still closed. The tremor in her grew stronger.

She twitched in his arms, then convulsed.

Abruptly he was frightened. "Anna? *Anna!*"

She was shaking now, rivers of mysterious energy pouring through her. Her eyes came open suddenly—

And Travis gazed into them.

It was a mistake. In that moment she was not Anna Blaise. She was not even a woman. . . .

Also by Robert Charles Wilson
Ask your bookseller for the books you have missed

MEMORY WIRE
GYPSIES
THE DIVIDE

A
Hidden
Place

Robert Charles Wilson

BANTAM BOOKS
NEW YORK • TORONTO • LONDON • SYDNEY • AUCKLAND

A HIDDEN PLACE

A Bantam Spectra Book / November 1986
3 printings through December 1989

ISBN 0-553-26103-7

Published simultaneously in the United States and Canada

―――――――――――――――――――――――――――――――

Bantam Books are published by Bantam Books, a division of
Bantam Doubleday Dell Publishing Group, Inc. Its trademark,
consisting of the words "Bantam Books" and the portrayal of
a rooster, is Registered in U.S. Patent and Trademark Office
and in other countries. Marca Registrada. Bantam Books,
666 Fifth Avenue, New York, New York 10103.

―――――――――――――――――――――――――――――――

PRINTED IN THE UNITED STATES OF AMERICA

KR   12 11 10 9 8 7 6 5 4 3

For Janet

Prelude:
Bone in California

Bone was the only one awake on the flatcar as the train labored out of the mountains and into the fog-choked valley, and it was Bone who saw the railroad cop.

He was only dimly aware of the danger. It was deep night, morning not far off, late in spring. The air was bitingly cold and damp. Bone was lucky; he had stolen a thick Navy pea coat the week before. He wore it now, pulled tight in one hand because he could not button it across his wide and bony rib cage. He had a hat, too; a thick woolen watch cap pulled down over his stubble hair so that it warmed his ears. Bone was lucky. But in that shivering predawn hour he was aware only of his acute discomfort, the convulsions that seemed to travel seismically from his feet up to the crown of his head. It was more than the cold; cold had never bothered him much; it was something else—a sickness.

He did not think about it in any detail. Thinking was difficult and unrewarding for him. Bone was notorious in the hobo jungles because he spoke so seldom, and because of his oversized joints and fleshless body. Even his name was not his own. It had been given to him on a similar train a long but (in Bone's mind) indefinite time ago. Most of the hoboes who rode the boxcars were emaciated. But Bone had gone beyond that: his huge ribs seemed to be fighting their way out of his parchment flesh; his elbows were sharp as flint axes; and when he bent you could watch the articulation of his knees, the patella sliding like some oiled mechanism in a hay baler or a forklift. They called him Bone, and he gave Bone as his name when he was asked.

Fatigue lay on him now like a drug, though he could not sleep. Fatigue and this new shuddering weakness. Electricity seemed to crawl over the surface of his skin. It reminded him of the time he had accepted from another tramp the offer of a swallow of muscatel. The liquor had burned like fire, and a little while later he had spasmed it all up again. Since then he had been careful to take only water.

The train slowed. He guessed they were approaching a railway yard, but a ground fog had risen up from the farm fields all around and had hidden the stars and the horizon. He sat up straighter at the thought of a railyard: in Bone's mind a railyard was a bright nexus of danger. It was then, abruptly, that he saw the cop, the beam of his flashlight flicking out of the mist to touch on Bone and the other figures asleep on the flatcar, the man's blue scissorbill cap cocked toward them avidly. The cop yelled something, but the train was still moving pretty fast; Bone was alarmed but figured there would be time to get away.

He woke up the other men one by one. In the difficult journey through the mountains he had learned some of their names. Benny and Joe, Deacon and Archibald, Campbell and Crawford. Some were singles, some moved in pairs or in temporary alliances of threes. They were uniformly dirty and they wore sack pants and rope belts just like Bone did. Bone woke the other hoboes by jostling them with his big knobby hands. Some, waking and seeing his angular Halloween face above them, involuntarily flinched away; but when he told them about the scissorbill they sat up frowning, furtively crouched.

Deacon Kenny and Bill Archibald came and squatted next to him. These two were a pair, and Deacon, a middle-aged man who said he was a meat-packer from Chicago, was the leader. Deacon was short and dense and tattooed and had an immense collection of snipes, unsmoked cigarette butts, which he hoarded and rationed as if they were a private treasure. Archibald, his buddy, was a lanky man who spoke in laconic, brief Southern drawls and carried Deacon's frying pan for him and would hold up a fragment of mirror so that Deacon could shave his face with a sliver of broken glass each morning. Deacon was an obsessive shaver; Archibald had a wispy tramp's beard that he would not cut off, though Deacon tugged on it and ragged him for it.

Bone had never shaved but didn't have a beard: he guessed it wasn't in him to grow one.

"Train'll go on through," Deacon said, nodding to himself. "The cop can't get on and we can't get off. It's safe."

"Is it?" Archie said. "Look there."

Bone stared where Archie was pointing. It was the cop's flashlight bobbing up and down, the cop chasing after them, still yelling, and now the train was slowing, too, was grinding to a stop. Deacon said, "Oh, shit."

At the sound of the brakes all the tramps leaped off the flatcar at once. It made Bone think of a man burning lice off his clothes with a lit cigarette, the way they jumped. Then Bone jumped, too. He landed crouched in the cindery gravel beside the track. The scissorbill was very close and he was shouting, and now—Bone could see them emerging from the fog— the yard bulls were running to join him. Suety, hostile men in dingy gray overalls.

"Bone!" Deacon was yelling. "This way! Bone! Run, dammit!"

The tramps were all scattering down the grade of the railway, through a scummy slough of water and into the foggy lettuce fields and the night. Bone moved to follow. But the seizure came then and he was down on the cold ground shaking. It was like a shiver that consumed his whole body. His awareness narrowed down to something like a speck, a black dot in a red emptiness. He was only distantly conscious when the railway cop pulled him up by the armpits, when the yard bulls—after a moment of disgusted commentary on his misshapen body—began to punch and kick him.

The blows came down like hard rain. Bone stared incuriously at his assailants. He had distanced himself from the pain. Cheated of a reaction, they hit and kicked him harder. Then—made queasy, perhaps, by the excesses he had inspired in them—they drifted away one by one; and the scissorbill, his cap askew now, muttered something Bone did not understand and pushed him with his foot down the stony grade and into the cold and stagnant water.

Bone lay in water up to his waist, his head cradled among the cinders and small stones, the steam of his breath rising up into the sky.

He listened for a while to the metallic shrieks as the railcars were coupled and uncoupled in the morning darkness.

He blinked his eyes and closed them, and time ceased.

He might have died. A dozen times before, a dozen different places, he had come as close. But then, as now, some kernel of intent had hardened within him. Waking, he felt it like a song inside him. It was diffuse and not specific; he could not tack it down with words. But he knew what it meant. It meant he would survive, would heal himself, would move on. He had been moving on, it seemed to him, all his life.

There were fingers, softly, at his neck, his chest, his feet.

He opened his eyes.

Gritty sunlight seared him. His body ached. He focused on the faces of Deacon and Archie above him. Deacon was stroking the stiff lapel of Bone's good blue pea coat.

Deacon grinned. "Bone is *awake*. See, Archie? Bone's gonna be okay."

Bone sat up.

Archie, who was angular and tall, said: "We would have taken the coat if you were dead, you know. And these shoes. We thought you might be dead."

"But he's *not* dead," Deacon said peevishly, his voice a throaty flat midwestern rasp. "Bone's *not* dead, are you, Bone? Bone, listen, there is a little jungle up the tracks. You want to come—Bone? Can you walk? Walk with old Deacon and Archie?"

Bone knew they had been trying to steal his clothes and that this was Deacon's way of apologizing for it. He felt no animosity toward them, but he wasn't sure he could stand up. The yard bulls had kicked him pretty hard. He had to try, though. He pulled himself erect. It was like a gantry standing up. He was six feet five inches tall—a hobo had measured him once, just to get the exact figure of it—and when he stood up he swayed like a tree. The small of his back hurt terribly and he put his hand back there. "Kidneys," Deacon said knowingly. "Yard bulls go for the kidneys. They always do. You'll be pissing blood for a day or two, Bone."

Bone thought he was probably right.

They moved on down the tracks. In daylight he was able to see that this was a tiny agricultural depot, locked in by oceans of lettuce and, far off, arbored grapes. The sun had burned off the mist and the day was hot and getting hotter. The heat came up off the cracked dry bed of the railroad right-of-way like a growing thing. He saw the jungle in the dis-

tance now as Deacon had said, a small con-
catenation of box huts and hovels where a river cut
through the broad flat valley and a stand of dusty
dogwoods had grown up.

Bone had never been here before, though he had
been many places like it. He knew he was not smart,
but something in him, some instinct, prevented him
from riding the same way twice. He wondered sometimes what he would do if he ran out of railroads,
but that had never happened; maybe, he thought, it
was impossible; maybe there were always more railroads, always more places like this. There certainly
seemed no end to it.

He wondered, too, what it was he was looking
for, what it was that pulled him with such a dire if
dimly sensed imperative. It was more than habit or
hunger. It was something he did not share with these
other men. Something for which he had not been
able to discover a name.

"I saw a man once," Deacon was saying, his
thin-soled shoes slapping against the packed earth,
"take a drink of muscatel and walk out the door of a
moving boxcar. I swear it, I saw him do that. Did he
live? I don't know. I guess it's possible. The things
people live through would surprise you. Like Bone
here. Beating like that would kill a normal man.
Yard bulls leave him in the ditch till somebody finds
him. City buries him . . . or they pitch him into the
river so he floats out to sea. There are more dead
tramps floating in the ocean than live ones riding
the rails: that's a fact. You go out some places the
water would be just thick with tramps. Like fish.
The tide brings them all together. That's what they
say."

"That's a crock of shit," Archie said.

"You don't know anything," Deacon said
calmly.

Bone had seen oceans, mountains, deserts so dry
they drew the moisture out of you and left you like a
cooked crab, all hard dry chitin and no meat. And

cold and hot. He had seen river valleys lush as rain forests, industrial towns black with coal smoke and battered by noise and poverty. It was all the same to him. There was a thing he wanted, and he had not found it. Something sweet, he thought, like music. Privately, he believed Deacon's story about the dead hoboes and wondered if he would end that way himself: Bone floating anonymously with the others, Bone merged into a vast human sea-wrack.

Deacon led him to a circle of charred stones under a tree, a blackened frying pan. "We have a little food," Deacon said. "You'd like that? Yeah? A little food?"

Bone nodded. He had not eaten for some days.

"Food," Deacon said, gratified.

Archibald sighed unhappily and began heating up a few chary slices of salt pork. There was a can, also, of concentrated soup.

Deacon sat down and Bone, grimacing in pain, crouched beside him. Deacon dug deep into the folds of his faded cotton shirt and brought forth one of his snipes—a "Sunday church snipe," Deacon called it; he had explained back on the flatcar that the best and longest snipes were the ones the churchgoers butted out just before services Sunday mornings. Bone didn't smoke; he shook his head, smiling to demonstrate his gratitude. He thought Deacon must be really sorry for trying to steal his coat. Deacon carefully repocketed the snipe and said, "You're the most ugly man I have ever seen but I like you. Bone, Deacon likes you."

Bone nodded, smiling industriously.

"Tonight," Deacon said, "we leave this pissant town. No work here. No use even looking. Ride away is about the best we can do."

"Bad place to camp," Archie put in.

"Bad cops," Deacon said. "That's the story here. You understand me, Bone? *Tonight*."

"Yes, Deacon," Bone said out loud. But he perceived that the sun was already on its way down, and the two men showed no signs of packing up. Move on, he thought, yes, that would be good.

Inside him, strange feelings stirred.

That night, for the first time, the feeling grew so strong in him that he thought it might drive him mad.

He woke up after Deacon and Archie and the rest of the hoboes in the meager encampment had fallen asleep. The fires were out and frying pans hung in the dogwood trees like Christmas decorations. It was dark, and the cold had come down again.

Bone sat up, shivering. He wasn't sure what had brought him awake. He gazed up at the nameless and unfamiliar constellations. This *feeling*, he thought. But maybe it was only hunger. Bone was big and the food he had begged from Deacon and Archie had only aroused his huge appetite.

He stood up, tiptoeing over Deacon where he was curled up in a moth-eaten Hudson's Bay blanket, and began to move silently and swiftly back along the train tracks. There was a crescent moon and Bone's night vision was very good. The rows of head lettuce stretched away to converge at the vanishing point, a horizon full of food. He boosted himself up a barbed-wire fence, ravaging the skin on his palms, and fell on the other side. The lettuce was all new growth but it didn't matter to Bone; he filled his mouth with green matter, swallowed, filled it again, again, until at last his hunger had abated some.

He sat back on his haunches, drooling.

He wasn't hungry anymore. And yet this other feeling persisted.

It was like his travel-on feeling, but more intense; as if his shuddering sickness had become a part of it and his hunger and his pain. It would not be still inside him.

His eyes twisted under his thick brow ridge. *What is it, what!*

He itched with an unfocused sense of urgency. That was when he heard the dogs.

Their baying broke the stillness like a knife. Bone crouched down instinctively, not breathing. But he was not in immediate danger: the sound was coming from the south, where the hobo jungle was.

A raid.

He had seen raids before. He knew how it was when the people came into a hobo camp with their pipes and shotguns. Once he had almost died in such a raid. His instinct was to run, to find a road or a train and get as far away from the violence as he could. But then he thought of Deacon and Archie sleeping and helpless back there and suddenly he was on his feet, running. His pulse beat in his ears, the air was cruel on his bloody hands, and he thought he might vomit up everything he had eaten. But he had to get back.

The southern end of the encampment had suffered first. The raiders were big men, farmers probably, in red-checked shirts and hunting jackets. A fire had started up in one of the cardboard hovels, embers flying up, the light of it making the violence seem slow and cinematic. The dogs had gone wild with the smoke and the stink of the jungle; they dove like ferrets into hovels to drag out screaming men. The farmers used their iron pipes on anyone who was slow or who resisted. It had happened so suddenly that those on the fringe of the encampment, like Deacon and Archie, were only just beginning to come awake.

Bone pulled on their arms, trying desperately to communicate some sense of urgency through the barrier of their fatigue. He remembered Deacon bragging that a real tramp could sleep anywhere, through anything—but the problem now was waking up. In the excitement Bone had forgotten all his words.

Archie sized up the situation quickly and managed to run a few paces ahead. Deacon stood up at last—the farmers were terribly close now—and his face contorted unhappily, as if he believed he might still be dreaming. Bone tugged him forward, but that was a mistake; Deacon cried out and fell over, his feet tangled in his own Hudson's Bay blanket.

Bone pulled him up. But it was too late. A farmer in an orange hunting jacket swung his pipe and caught Deacon hard on the arm. Deacon shrieked and fell back. The farmer raised his pipe again, and Bone perceived that the man would kill Deacon if the blow were allowed to fall. To prevent it, Bone grasped the farmer's right arm at its fullest extension and twisted until it snapped—a thing he had not realized he could do. The farmer gazed at Bone very briefly, his face gone white with shock and confusion; then he stumbled back, screaming.

Deacon was weeping with pain but managed to scuttle forward with his rucksack in his good hand. Archie helped him up, gap-jawed: "Deacon," he said, "Deacon, you see what that big man *did*? Jesus!"

"Go," Deacon sobbed, "just for Christ's sakes go!"

Two more of the farmers came up on the heels of the first, and before Bone could decently run he had to swing out his long arms with their fists like weights so that these two men fell down also, one of them unconscious and one almost certainly dead. A sort of collective moan rose up from the raiders.

This time Bone did not need to be goaded. He ran, keeping abreast of his friends. The fires roared behind him.

"Boxcar!" Deacon shouted. "See!"

A long, ponderous freight was just pulling out of the yards. The yard bulls and the railway cops had all congregated down by the hobo jungle; the open door of the boxcar gaped like a broken tooth. The three of them ran to catch it, Deacon favoring his injured shoulder. Before they reached it, though, a scissorbill stepped up from the shadows in the gully, and he was carrying a shotgun.

Deacon and Archie fell to their knees. Bone didn't think about it at all. Reflexively, he let his momentum carry him forward as the railroad cop leveled the gun; he was faster than the man's reaction time and was able to duck under the line of fire before the big muzzles of the gun erupted into the night. Then his broad bony hand was on the cop's face, twisting it back, snapping vertebrae; the scissorbill fell backward into the scummy slough, dead before the idea of death could enter his mind.

Deacon helped Bone up into the boxcar. There were scraps of straw in the corners and the smell of cattle. They would be cold again tonight, Bone thought bleakly. But that hardly mattered now.

Deacon gazed back at the body of the scissorbill as the train picked up speed.

"He's meat," Deacon marveled. "Christ God, Archie, you were right."

Archie looked at Bone from his recessed eyes and said nothing.

They slid the doors closed as the train accelerated into the night.

Deacon, still favoring his left arm, slapped Bone on the back.

"Stick with us, kid," he said. "Stick with old Deacon and Archie."

The next day there were mountains again, and snow in the night. Bone huddled in his pea coat—it was torn now—and listened to Deacon and Archie swap tales about how it had been in Bakersfield and Terre Haute and Klamath Falls and how it felt to be crossing the Hump again. Deacon brought out a bottle of muscatel and the two of them drank until their conversation blurred and Bone could no longer understand them. They gave him little quizzical sidelong glances, called him "Buddy" and "Good Friend Bone" and were careful to offer him what they had, more profusely when they were reassured that he would not accept. Eventually they fell asleep.

Bone sat in the open door of the boxcar, the cold wind tearing at him. There was a pulsing in him, much stronger than it had been before. He could feel it.

For the first time it made words inside him—the ghosts of words.

Here I am, find me. Find me, here I am.

The train roared down the eastern spine of the Continental Divide, and Bone felt the same unfamiliar strength rising up in him, the strength that had allowed him to kill all those men back at the railyard. He was focused now. Aimed. For the first time in Bone's memory he knew where he was going.

Here I am. Find me.

The clear, high song of it was unmistakable. At last he understood.

Bone was coming.

Chapter One

The municipality of Haute Montagne stood at the junction of the Fresnel River and the railway, its water tower and its huge granaries erupting from the prairie like blocks of basalt from an eroded sea floor. Once, not long ago, the town had aspired to be a city.

It still had a little of city in it. There was the main street, Lawson Spur, or simply The Spur, which was blacktopped and lined with concrete sidewalks dazzlingly white in the noonday sun, which boasted the big Bingham's Hardware Store and J. C. Penney's and Times Square Lunch, all fronted in dusty yellow brick; and there was the trolley that ran on embedded rails from the switching yard down The Spur to the granaries farther south. Everyone agreed that those were big-city conveniences. Once they had been accepted as harbingers of greater things.

But Haute Montagne remained a small town in its artful cultivation of box elders and bur oaks, in its side streets on which the pavement gave way quickly to cobbles or pressed dirt, in its gabled clapboard houses with high dormers and big front stoops that looked so invitingly shady when high summer lay on the town like liquid metal. It was a small town by virtue of its silences at noon and midnight, and the distances the big trains traveled before they arrived hissing at the depot. The prairie vastnesses had made of the town an island, isolated, proud in its isolation, set apart from the chaos that had so lately descended on the country at large.

But the town was not in any real way safe, no safer than New York or Los Angeles or Chicago, and perhaps that unacknowledged wisdom made its decline the more galling. Haute Montagne ("where the railroad meets the wheatfield") might once have wanted to be a city, but that ambition had died—or at least had been set aside, like the hope chest of a young woman destined for spinsterhood—in the Depression that had come like a bad cold and stayed to become something worse, some lingering if not fatal disease. The granaries had laid off much of the town's male population; the trains stopped less often; dust and drought had withered too much fertile land. The noon silences became profounder. Midnights were interminable. There was a sense, never explicit, of some even darker eventuality hovering like an army of locusts beyond the indefinite horizon—biding its time.

Travis Fisher had some feeling of that when he stepped off the eastbound train and onto the whitewashed boards of the Haute Montagne depot with July like a haze in the air.

He had been tempted to stay on the train all the way to wherever it went, New York, Maine, just sit and watch the miles pass away like unremembered dreams. His ticket was paid up only this far, though, and he had change of a dollar in his pocket for money and no real choice. He climbed off the pullman car into an immense summer silence and withdrew from his shirt pocket the hand-drawn map his Aunt Liza had sent him in the mail. South down The Spur to Lambeth, west on Lambeth to DeVille, number 120. In truth he was a little afraid of this new place, but he was nineteen years old and had carried a grown man's responsibilities since the year he had turned twelve, and so he straightened his shoulders and picked up his bag and began walking. The canvas bag contained a change of clothes and a photograph of his mother. It was not heavy.

There were old men and young men side-by-side on the public benches in front of the train station, and they all looked at Travis with an eloquent incuriosity. His footsteps on the pavement were loud in his ears. At the corner of Lambeth and Spur he should have turned west, but he saw the Times Square Lunch with its wide glass windows and realized at once how hungry he was. He bought a dime western at a newsstand and let himself gratefully into the cool shade of the diner. There were three men at a side table but nobody at the long Formica-topped lunch bar.

He ordered himself a hamburger and a Coke. The hamburger was a slab of broiled beef and the Coke came in a big soda-fountain glass with condensation on it like dew. The waitress was young, dark-haired, small-breasted under her uniform, and she gave him a series of covert glances. When she brought over the side of french fries she said, "You must be Travis Fisher."

"Trav," he said automatically, only then realizing how odd it was that she should know his name. "How did you—?"

"Relax," she said. She put her elbows on the counter. "I'm Nancy. Nancy Wilcox. My mom knows your Aunt Liza through the Baptist Women." She rolled her eyes to demonstrate her attitude toward the Baptist Women. "I guess just about everybody knew you were coming in today."

He was not sure he was pleased to hear that. But she was pretty, so he thanked Nancy Wilcox anyway and said he hoped he'd see her around.

"Probably you will," she said. "Mom and Liza Burack aren't exactly close, but they move in all the same circles. High-minded, you know: church com-

mittees, temperance league. Translation: busybodies."
She winked and turned away, flipping her long dark
hair out of her eyes. Travis gazed at her a moment
before directing his attention to the dime western
and the hamburger.

The hamburger was satisfying, the magazine
less so. He was an attentive reader, but today the he-
roes seemed too operatic, the violence perversely too
affecting. Six-guns blazed, blood poured, justice (except in the "continued" serial) triumphed. But he
could not help thinking of his mother and of the ug-
liness of her death and his impotent rage at it, so
after a while he put down his thirty cents on the
shiny Formica and left.

Haute montagne was French for "high mountain,"
his mother had told him, but whatever Frenchman
named the place must have been drunk or blind. His
aunt's house, 120 DeVille, stood on the highest plot
of land in town, where the prairie rose in a kind of
swell for thirty or forty feet before sloping away to
the bank of the Fresnel River and the railway bed.
The house itself was old but had once been fine: two
stories plus a small garret with oculus windows
overlooking the town; but the wooden siding was
textured with paint curls and the weather had got
into the dormers. Yellow curtains were drawn
against the sunlight.

Travis had not been there since he was six years
old.

He knocked three times on the rim of the screen
door and then Aunt Liza answered.

Liza was his mother's older sister, in her middle
fifties now, respectable in a print sack dress, and she
opened the door and looked at Travis with a mixture
of pity and suspicion that he recognized instantly
over the gulf of years. She had aged some. There
were lines in her high pale forehead; she wore a pair
of silver-rimmed glasses with a bifocal half. Her figure was undefined, rounded. But she was unmistak-

ably Liza Burack. "Well, Travis," she said. "Well, come on in."

His own reluctance to cross that threshold was surprisingly strong. But he shouldered his bag through the door and into the ticking silence.

Persian rugs. Mantle clocks.

In the whitewashed kitchen, an electric fan purred.

"Creath," Liza said, "Travis is here."

Creath Burack was the man Liza had married ("A steady man," she always told Travis's mother; he operated the Haute Montagne ice plant): immobile in an armchair, overalls riding up his big belly, hair thin, he stood up just long enough to shake Travis's hand. His grip was huge, painful.

"You start work tomorrow," Creath Burack said.

Travis nodded. Liza said, "Well, you probably want to see your room."

She led him up a flight of carpeted stairs to a room with naked floorboards and whitewashed walls, empty but for a narrow brass bed and a pine dresser. Travis raised a yellowing sash and was able to see an arc of the river, the railway trestle, the horizon like a line drawn against the sky.

Something moved, lightly, in the attic room above him.

He looked at Liza. She avoided his eyes. "We have another roomer up there," she said, "but you wouldn't know about that. You'll meet her at supper, I suppose."

"Yes, ma'am," Travis said.

She stood in the doorway and her eyes hardened.

"Travis, I want you to know there was never any question of whether you should come here or not."

"No, ma'am."

"Oh, Creath might have raised a word or two. But he just likes his privacy. No, blood is thicker, I told him. Soon as I heard about your mama's tragedy

I said, well, we'll take in Trav, and maybe you can get him a place down at the iceworks. I don't guess it was your fault what happened to Mary-Jane. Her *own* fault . . . if any, if any." This last because of the look Travis had given her. "But I want you to know. This is not the kind of household you might be accustomed to. We have standards of conduct. And Creath, he doesn't like a lot of noise. Best you keep quiet around him, Travis, you understand? And not ask too many questions."

Her face was shaded with old pain.

"Yes, ma'am," Travis said.

She closed the door, and he gazed at the cream-colored walls.

Dusk came, and he had not switched on the single overhead light when Liza Burack called him down for supper.

The dining-room table was heaped high with food. He remembered this, too, about his Aunt Liza, the way she went all out cooking for people, not so much generosity as compensation, as if the sheer weight of food could disguise some hidden inadequacy. Creath was already seated at the table, a massive blank weight, as Liza delivered a white china bowlful of mashed potatoes, a brimming gravy boat.

"Looks fine," Travis said. "Mama always admired your cooking very much, Aunt Liza."

"Just you sit down," Liza said nervously. "The proof's in the eating, Travis."

It was as if he was still six years old.

"Lot of work went into setting this table," Creath said; and Travis thought, yes, *her* work, but it was obvious he meant the ice plant. "Lot of time, lot of work. Hope you appreciate that."

"Yessir."

"Nothing comes cheap." Creath's eyes were unfocused and Travis guessed he had said these things many times. "You work for what you get in this life, you understand that, Travis?"

"Sir."

"That may have been the problem with your mother. Expect too much without wanting to work for it. Well, we all know where that path inclines, I guess."

I am a guest in his home, Travis thought, teeth clenched. I cannot say what I think. But he looked at Creath Burack with a barely restrained loathing.

"Creath," Liza said, gently warning.

"It's only what the boy has to hear. Better he should know it now than come to it hard later on."

Liza, silent, delivered a steaming pot roast to the table. The heat and humidity of it filled the dining room; Travis felt a drop of sweat travel down his chest. His stomach felt shriveled.

"Because," Creath went on, "and I say this honestly, I won't accept second-best from you down at the plant. Some might say it was favoritism, my hiring you on at all. Now I don't believe that. I don't think it is un-Christian to help a family member in need. The opposite. But charity does not extend to indulgence. That's all I'm trying to put across. Work is what is required. Maybe things have been easy for you before. But the sad truth is that they will not be easy now."

Travis said quietly, "When Mama was sick I hired the men to harvest. I drove a tractor, and a team of horses when we sold the tractor. And when we couldn't hire hands I took what I could of the harvest myself."

"Well," Creath said, "we know what the upshot of that was, don't we?"

"Creath," Liza said quickly, "will you give us the blessing?"

Creath muttered a may-God-be-thanked and was reaching for the boiled peas when the Buracks' other roomer came down the stairs.

She had been silent on the carpeted steps and Travis was startled at the shadow. He had forgotten about the attic room. He stood up from the table, a gesture his mother had taught him was polite when a woman enters.

There was a brief, tense silence.

"Travis Fisher," Liza said distantly, "this is Anna Blaise."

He stared at her a long moment before he remembered to take her hand. "Meet you," he said clumsily, and she made a movement like a curtsy.

He knew he was being impolite, but she was shockingly beautiful. She was young, Travis thought, maybe his own age, but the longer he looked at her the less certain he was. She was radiant and smooth-skinned but her eyes contained depths he did not associate with youth. Her face was round. Her hair was blond and rough-cut and tied back behind her with an alluring carelessness. She gazed at the floor as if uncertain what she ought to do or say; but beneath this shyness there was an inference of great poise, an economy of motion. Travis felt clumsy next to her.

"Why don't we all sit down," Liza said flatly.

"Yes," Anna said, and her voice was a match for the rest of her, calm and modulated, like the playing of a distant flute. She sat down opposite Liza Burack and made the table a symmetry.

For a time, no one spoke. The rattle of their cutlery was loud in the silence.

Covertly, Travis watched the girl eat. She kept her eyes downcast, took small portions, used her knife and fork daintily. It occurred to him to marvel that the Buracks had taken in another boarder. He remembered his aunt and uncle being intensely private people. Family people. Times were bad, he thought; they must need the money. But where had she come from?

"I'm from Oklahoma," he ventured to say. "Near Beaumont."

Her eyes were on him very briefly.

"Yes," she said. "The Buracks told me you were coming."

"You from around here?"

"Not too far," she said.

"Working in town?"

"I work here," she said. "In the house. I do sewing. I—"

"For Christ's sake," Creath said, "leave her alone."

Travis was mortified. "I'm sorry," he said.

Anna Blaise smiled and shrugged.

Something wrong here, Travis thought. Odd and wrong. But he went about his eating.

"Didn't make but a dent in that pot roast," Liza said with a sigh when they were finished. She rose, moaning a little, and picked up the big china platter. Anna stood up unbidden and took her own plate, Travis's, Creath's.

There was the sound of clattering in the kitchen, a gush of running water.

Creath withdrew a big Virginia cigar and made a ceremony of lighting it. He looked at Travis for a time over the glowing tip.

"Don't think I don't know what's happening," the older man said.

"Sir?"

"Keep your voice down." He sighed out a plume of smoke. "You think I don't know. But I do. The heat, the summer—and you look at her—you have *feelings*. But there will be none of that in this house. Don't answer me! This is not a conversation. This is the rules. She is way out of your class, Travis Fisher."

Travis groped for an answer, astonished. But before he could speak Liza had come back from the kitchen with syrupy wedges of blackberry pie laid out on china plates.

"My!" Creath said expansively. "This *is* a treat."

* * *

It was round about midnight when Nancy Wilcox walked past the Burack house on DeVille.

She was coming from the open field where the railway trestle crossed the Fresnel River, where Greg Morrow had left her when she refused to let him put his hand up her skirt.

Greg was a pretty rough character, oldest son of a granary worker. He owned a decade-old Tin Lizzie with a blown cylinder in which he squired around whichever female he could talk into a ride. He chewed tobacco and he used what the Baptist Women called "gutter language." Precisely the kind of date her mother would disapprove of . . . which was maybe why Nancy had agreed to go with him in the first place. His crudity was kind of fascinating.

Ultimately, however, Greg was not the person Nancy wanted to *do it* with. If she had had any doubts, the events at the trestle had settled them. She was not a prude; she had read about free love in a book by H. G. Wells before her mother caught her with it (and had the small volume deleted from the town library); she had even *done it* a couple of times before, with a boy named Marcus whose family had since moved west.

But not with Greg. Greg seemed to think it was owed him, something that was his by right, and Nancy did not feel obliged to encourage him in this delusion. So he had kicked her out of the Lizzie down by the trestle, which made her a little nervous because lately there had been hoboes gathering there; she had seen their fires flickering in the angular darkness under the railway bridge. But she just walked steady and kept her head about her and pretty soon she was back among the streetlights and the box elders. She would catch righteous hell for getting home so late, of course. But in a way she was glad. She liked this time of night, liked to listen to the town ticking and cooling after a blast-furnace July day like this one had been. The midnight breeze on her face was soothing; the trees chattered to themselves in what she liked to imagine was a secret language.

She gazed up at the gray outline of the Burack house against the stars.

In the darkness it appeared to be just what that Mrs. Burack obviously imagined it was: a sturdy keystone in Haute Montagne's social structure. You couldn't see the peeling paint, the rain gutters clotted with mulch. Nancy smiled to herself, thinking of what her mother always said about the Buracks: something *odd* there, something definitely *odd,* and that girl in the attic!—about as talkative as a deaf-mute, and a lot less wholesome.

Nancy peered up at the attic room and saw a faint light flicker there, like fox fire behind the sun-yellowed blinds.

"Strange," she said to herself. . . .

And there was that Fisher boy, now, too, the one who had stopped by the diner this afternoon. There had been rumblings about his situation, a fatherless family, mother a runabout, hints of some darker truth. But that could have been just the Baptist Women's rumor mill at work, Nancy thought, grinding a very modest kernel of truth. He had seemed nice. If distracted. He had left his magazine at the diner. Nancy had gazed a long time at the cover of it: horses, guns, a range of purple mountains. *He is from far away.*

She let the night air carry back her hair. She felt like a shadow sometimes, blowing through these night streets. Time carried her on like a cork on a wave—she was already eighteen—and she had lately become desperate with wondering: where was she bound? She sometimes dreamed of mountains (like the mountains on Travis Fisher's pulp magazine), of cities, of oceans. She shivered, gazing up at the old Burack house.

She wondered what sort of person Travis Fisher was, and what he dreamed about.

In the attic room, the light flared brighter.

Travis lay in bed, exhausted but helplessly awake, an uneasy excitement running in him like a river. He felt the unfamiliar pressure of the mattress under him. He had covered his nakedness with a single sheet, because it was summer and all the heat in the house traveled up to these high narrow rooms and was retained there. The attic, he thought, must be sizzling.

She doesn't make much noise.

Anna Blaise, he thought, tasting the name: Anna Blaise, Anna Blaise.

He had heard, during the long evening, the restless treadle of her sewing machine, her radio playing briefly. Then silence. Later on, the quick compression of bedsprings.

The house made its own sounds, sighs and moans. Travis had propped open the window with a hardware-store expansion screen and every once in a while a breeze picked up the corner of the sheet. Sleep, he thought, and it was a prayer now: sleep, oh, sleep.

Shortly after midnight he heard footsteps on the stairway beyond his door.

Slow, heavy footsteps coming up from below. Aunt Liza didn't carry that much bulk—it could only be Creath.

This time of night! Travis thought.

The footsteps paused outside his door and then proceeded upward.

Strange, Travis thought.

And now they were over his head. *Creath, for sure.*

A brief, low burr of conversation. Anna's voice like faraway music, Creath's like the grumble of some rusted old machine.

The repetitive complaint of the bedsprings.

Jesus God Almighty, Travis thought, that poor little girl!—and he covered his ears with his pillow. .

Chapter Two

The evenings were essentially the same for the next week and a half: an elaborate ritual dinner, Anna's opacity and silences, Creath's clenched-fist approach to conversation. Later there might be radio, Creath lighting up a cigar and occupying the parlor easy chair for the duration of "Amos & Andy" or Ed Wynn or, Sundays, Father Coughlin's "Golden Hour of the Little Flower." Then everybody eased upstairs to hot and insulated beds, and Travis, if he stayed awake, might hear Creath tiptoeing into the attic room . . . not always, but too often. It forced Travis to look at his Aunt Liza's nervous flutters with a greater degree of sympathy: she knows, he thought, she *must* know.

Weekdays Creath drove him down to the ice plant before dawn. The thought of all that ice had made Travis imagine the plant might be a nice place in which to endure this long summer. But—although he did sometimes enter the cool length of the storeroom where block ice lay stacked like uncut fragments from some fairy-tale diamond mine—most of his work was in the tin shed where the refrigerating machinery roared and thumped, perversely twenty degrees hotter than the outside air. The work he did was mostly lifting and cleaning, and he quickly learned that the other men who worked here, mechanics and loaders and drivers, considered him a liability, contemptible, the boss's nephew. He ate bagged lunches alone in a weedy field beyond the loading dock, staring into the brown Fresnel River. The ice industry was doomed, Creath had said, victim of the goddamned Kelvinator. It might survive a while longer here in Haute Montagne, but orders were already way down for this time of year. Travis found the knowledge perversely consoling. The work itself was tedious and frustrating, and when the frustration threatened to overwhelm him he decided to ask Nancy Wilcox for a date.

That Friday evening after work he told Creath to let him off at the corner of Lambeth and The Spur. Creath accelerated his Model A pickup through a yellow light and said, "Your aunt will have dinner ready. You not hungry?"

"I'll get something down here." He avoided the older man's eyes. "Maybe see a movie."

"Waste of money," Creath said, but he downshifted the truck and slowed long enough to allow Travis to leap out.

There were still a couple of hours of daylight left. The sky was a powdery blue, the shadows stark and angular. He went directly to the diner. Nancy Wilcox had not been on his mind nearly as much as Anna Blaise . . . but Anna Blaise was a mystery, at once violated and aloof, as unapproachable as a cat. Nancy was someone he might talk to.

She was there in the murky interior of the diner. An overhead fan stirred the air. The tables were all busy and there was a second waitress on duty. He sat at the counter, smiled, ordered the chuck steak and a cole slaw side and wondered how to approach her.

He was not shy with women, not in the ordinary sense, but he had had only a pittance of real experience. Back home only Millie Gardner, the neighbor girl, had spoken much with him, and by the time Travis left Millie was just turning twelve and had already begun to grow aloof. Other than that he had talked to his mother, his schoolteachers, a couple of girls doing what they obviously perceived as a kind of distasteful social work when he was left conspicuously alone at school functions. It was humiliating; but there were others who were, in a way, worse off; who were ostracized for some mental or physical deformity and not solely on account of their family situation. And although he had often enough prayed that it was otherwise, Travis knew, at least, that he was not despised altogether for himself.

But that was back home. This was a new place. Here it was still possible that Travis could expect some of what he had so far been pointedly denied. Nobody knew him here, and that simple fact was as tantalizing as a promise.

He lingered over the steaming plate of food, which he did not much want, killing time. There was no good opportunity to talk. Nancy moved deftly between the tall aluminum coffee urn and the soda fountain, balanced plates on her arms, pinned table orders on the silver carousel for the kitchen to pick up. He watched her pluck a strand of steamed black hair out of her eyes and thought: well, this is impossible. Nevertheless he lingered over his coffee and asked for refills. The hot black coffee made his heart beat faster. His eyes were on her constantly. And he thought: she at least notices me here.

In time the tables began to empty, the humidity eased. She filled his cup for the third time and said, "Eight o'clock."

He looked at her, stupefied.

She put her elbows on the counter. "That's when I get off. Eight o'clock. That's what you want to know, isn't it?"

"I guess it is."

"I've seen the Cagney film at the Rialto but there's a new one at the Fox. *Jewel Robbery*. William Powell and Kay Francis. You like William Powell?"

"He's pretty good."

Travis had seen three moving pictures in his life.

She smiled. "Well, I guess I'm going over there after work."

"I guess so am I," he said.

She surprised him by stopping off at the Haute Montagne Public Library and slipping three fat volumes into the night depository: a Hemingway novel, a book on astronomy, and something by a German named Carl Gustav Jung.

Travis said, "You read all that?"

"Uh-huh." She gave him that smile again: it was harder now, defiant, and he guessed she must have been ribbed about her reading. "Don't you read?"

"Magazines mostly." In fact he had had a fair amount of time for reading in the long winters back home. She would already have seen the dime western; and he was not prepared to admit to the stacks of stolen, borrowed, or dearly bought science fiction and adventure pulps he had ploughed through. Not when she was dumping Carl Gustav Jung into the night slot.

They moved along the darkened sidewalks back toward Lawson Spur and the Fox Theater.

There was a short line at the ticket box and Travis saw other girls there, high-school girls or just older, and observed how they looked at Nancy Wilcox, the crabbed sidelong glances and covert stares. It was a phenomenon he recognized, and he thought: What is there about her? He paid for two tickets and they sat together in the mezzanine, gazing down silently for a time at the plush velvet curtains over the screen while a fat woman played overtures on the Wurlitzer. Travis felt the girl's warm pressure next to him. She smelled good, he thought, some perfume and just a lingering indication that she had put in a long day in a hot restaurant. It was a wholesome smell. It aroused him and it made him nervous: he wondered what was expected of him, whether he should hold her hand or keep to himself. He did not want to insult her. Then the lights flickered down, the organ hissed into silence, the movie started. It was one of those cocktail-and-evening-gown movies, everybody pronouncing calculated bon mots in rooms that seemed to Travis too impossibly large and lushly furnished. He watched in a sort of dazed incomprehension, and when Nancy pressed her body toward him he intertwined his arm with hers and they were, at least, that close.

After the movie they went for Cokes.

The Wilcox girl's hair had strayed down in front of her eyes again. She probed at the ice with her straw and said, "You don't go out much, do you?"

"Is it so obvious?"

"No, Travis. Nothing wrong. Just you seemed a bit uncomfortable is all."

Travis was carefully silent.

She said, "I guess you were kind of a misfit back where you came from."

"Your mother told you that?"

"Said as much, I guess, but that's not what I mean. I mean the way you move, the way you talk. Very, I don't know, *wary*. Like something's going to jump out at you."

"A misfit," he said. "I guess that's about it."

"I'm a misfit. Did you know that?" She sipped her Coke again.

"Those books?"

"Partly. Nobody reads in this town. Miss Thayer who works at the library, *she* doesn't even read. But that's not all of it." She said, as if offering a vital confidence, "I don't get along with people."

"I know what that's like," Travis said.

"Partly it's my mother. She makes a profession out of being righteous. She believes the world is going straight to hell. So I guess the pressure's on me to live up to all that. I'm supposed to be perfect—a saintly little female Imitation of Christ. I guess I just, ah, cracked." She laughed. "She's so *afraid* of everything, you know, Travis? Afraid and suspicious. And I'm the opposite."

He smiled distantly. "Never afraid?"

"Not of what she's afraid of."

"What's she afraid of?"

Nancy gazed out the big window of the diner. It was way past dark now. All the cars had their lights on. "Love. Sex. Politics. Dirty words." She waved her hand. "All that."

"Oh," Travis said, taken aback.

"Are you afraid of those things?" She was staring at him now.

"Hell, no," he said, hoping it was not a lie.

But she laughed and seemed to loosen up. "No," she said, "no, I don't guess you are." And she drained her Coke. "Walk me home?"

At the corner of the street where she lived Nancy turned and touched his arm. "I don't want my mother to see us. She'll be on to us soon enough anyway. You can kiss me if you want, Travis."

The offer surprised him. He was clumsy but earnest.

She nodded thoughtfully then, as if she had entered some particularly revealing notation in a private notebook. His hands lingered on her.

"One day," she said, "you have to tell me the truth about it."

"About what?"

"You know. Where you came from. What happened there." She hesitated. "Your mother."

"She was a very fine woman," Travis said.

"*Is* that the truth?"

He stepped away from her. "Yes."

Chapter Three

Three Sundays after Travis arrived in Haute Montagne, Liza Burack made up her special millefeuilles for the Baptist Women's bake sale.

The day was dusty and hot, as all the days had been that parched summer, and the baked goods were set up on the lawn of the First Baptist, in the shadow of the high quatrefoil stained-glass windows which were the building's only adornment. Reverend Shaffer had brought out the big sprucewood tables and Mrs. Clawson had provided drop cloths. The edibles were displayed thereon—quite artistically, Liza thought, the candies and pastries in attractive circles like tiny works of art. Shirley Croft's almond cake had been given, as usual, pride of place. Shirley herself stood guard against the circling flies, flailing with an elder branch and wearing the sort of vigilant expression her late husband might have displayed to the Germans at the Battle of the Somme. Faye Wilcox was at one end of the table, Liza at the other, like the two polarities of an electrical cell.

I will just drift down, Liza thought. After all. Appearances. And what with the way things were going . . . well.

She moved lightly past the creamhorns and butter cookies.

She liked these times best, she thought, all the people around her, the aimless chatter. It was like being pulled in many directions at once. If she closed her eyes she could almost imagine herself floating, the baked goods like scattered islands in an ocean of afternoon, the heat on her like a benediction. Everything condensed in this minute point of experience.

But such ideas worried her (her thoughts strayed too easily these days) and she forced herself to stay on course: Faye Wilcox, she instructed herself, talk to Faye.

The Wilcox woman was heavy and hostile. Her arms were laced under her bosom. It looked for all the world as if her body were some unpleasant excrescence that had leaked, unavoidably, into public sight. Well, Liza thought, it's that outfit, hardly better than a sack. But who am I to talk? She glanced with momentary embarrassment at herself. Her cornflower dress was streaked with white from the morning's baking. She had neglected to change. And had she combed her hair? Lord, Lord, where was her *mind?*

"Lovely afternoon, Liza." It was Reverend Shaffer, cruising across the broad green church lawn. He was a young man and there was, Liza thought, something almost feminine about him, such a contrast with the Reverend Kinney who had died just two autumns ago. Reverend Shaffer used the pulpit to deliver obscure parables, to pose questions; Reverend Kinney had been more concerned with answers. It was, Liza thought, too symptomatic of the changes that had overtaken the nation, the town, her life. But she mustn't dwell on that. "It *is* nice," she said.

The flies were intense, the heat debilitating, there were no customers.

"Everybody loves your napoleons," the Reverend said.

"Mille-feuilles," Liza said automatically.

"Pardon me?"

"Mother always called them mille-feuilles. Mary-Jane—that's my sister—my, how she loved those pastries! She was always pestering Mother. 'Make up your mill-fills, Mama, make up your mill-fills!' She ate and ate and never got fat. Not like me. . . ."

"And how is your sister?" the Reverend asked, puzzled.

"Dead," Liza said. "Dead and, I presume, in hell."

Reverend Shaffer frowned. "The judgment's not ours to make, Mrs. Burack."

"You didn't know Mary-Jane, Reverend. Please—take a mille-feuille."

But the Reverend only gazed at her coolly and drifted away.

How different it had been when she was a girl. In those days there had been virtue and vice, distilled and pure essences between which one might choose. Not this muddying, not this terrible confusion. Liza straightened her spine and gazed at the Wilcox woman—Nancy's mother.

"Love your butter tarts," she said.

Faye Wilcox looked at her as if from a great distance. "You haven't even tried one, Liza dear."

"Oh, I couldn't. But they're so beautiful. Just so perfect."

"Thank you," Faye said.

"Did you see my mille-feuilles?"

"Lovely as always."

She is so hard, Liza thought sadly. Hard as granite. At one time, of course, they had been friends—allies, at least; wary, but with the same goals before them. In those days (it would have been three years ago: she remembered the annual picnic, "Summer 1929" printed on the invitation cards) Liza had been the leading light of the Baptist Women. It was Liza who had organized the letter campaign to the public school board concerning their thoughtless promotion of the Darwin Theory in the high-school textbooks; it was Liza who had chaired the Temperance Committee. Everyone agreed that without Liza Burack the Baptist Women would have been a vastly less effectual organization.

But then things had begun to happen. Things over which she had no control. That Blaise girl had moved in. Creath began to act strangely. Mary-Jane had come down sick off in Oklahoma, and there was no way Liza could visit, not merely on account of the distance but because of the sort of woman Mary-Jane had allowed herself to become.

The upshot of it all was: Liza faded. She had heard other people use that expression. *Faded.* It was an odd word. It made her think of flowers left too long in a vase. She thought with some astonishment: *I have faded.*

And of course Faye Wilcox had stepped into the vacuum Liza had left; and now it was Faye who organized the letter campaigns, the library boycotts; now it was Faye everyone looked to for guidance.

But Faye had her own Achilles' heel, Liza thought, suppressing a certain vindictive pleasure. She had that daughter of hers, who was quite notorious. Faye herself complained sometimes, though she was shrewd enough to blame it on the schools. . . .

And now, Liza thought, Nancy Wilcox and Travis Fisher were going together.

"I suppose," Liza said, "you've heard about Nancy and my sister's boy?"

Faye adopted a stern equanimity. Her eyes were steely, buried in small effusions of flesh. "I know they've been seen together."

"My goodness, hasn't Nancy talked it over with you?"

"Nancy is not inclined to do that."

"Faye, that girl doesn't appreciate what you do for her."

Faye relaxed a little. "Indeed she does not. I'm sometimes grateful Martin isn't alive to hear the back talk she gives me. It would break his heart."

"You deserve better."

"It's in the Lord's hands," Faye Wilcox said primly. "And Travis? Have you had any trouble—?"

"Creath says he is unhappy at work. But no real trouble, no, thank God."

"The times . . ." Faye Wilcox said.

"Oh, yes."

"Of course, the boy's mother . . ."

"Tragic." Liza added, "I mean, her death."

"One wonders if tendencies are inherited."

"He *is* a hard worker, in spite of what Creath says. He seems quite stable here. The influence of the home counts for so much, don't you think?"

Faye nodded grudgingly and brushed the air above her butter tarts. Flies buzzed.

"Still, it could be worse," Liza said. "The two of them."

Faye Wilcox gazed across the lawn, the baking asphalt street, her eyes unfocused.

"It could be," she admitted.

There, Liza thought. It had been decided. In that strained admission, a truce. Nancy and Travis would be allowed to continue seeing each other.

It was, for both Liza and Faye, the best of the meager alternatives. Faye had accepted it . . . grudgingly, no doubt, for it returned to Liza a measure of control.

Now, Liza thought, now what does *this* mean? What does this portend for the future?

"Those tarts just look so good," Liza said.

Faye held one out to her by the paper wrapper, an offering. "*Please.*"

"Thank you," Liza said, biting deeply into the pastry.

The ripe sweetness of it exploded in her mouth.

Trav and Nancy made Friday night a regular thing. Twice, as the month crawled toward September, he met her on Saturday as well. When there was nothing at the Fox or the Rialto they walked up The

Spur toward the railway depot or out to the wide, grassy fields where the Fresnel ran beyond the town. Nancy knew where the wild strawberry patches were, though the dry season had yielded very few berries. And, slowly, Travis had come to know Nancy.

He liked her. He harbored an admiration for her frankness, her outrageous willingness to defy convention. She had quite consciously put herself in a position Travis had long occupied against his will: outsider, loner—"misfit" was the word she liked to use. And that fascinated him. But it disturbed him, too, the lightheartedness of it, as if she were playing a game with something really quite dangerous, something she did not altogether understand . . . compromising her femininity with this reckless curiosity. He liked her, but in a strange way he was also afraid of her.

They had come to the strawberry fields again. The sun was going down now, the day's heat beginning to abate, darkness rising from the eastern horizon beyond the ruin of a shack where, Nancy said, an eccentric railway switchman had once lived. The town was not far away—the train depot was hardly more than a quarter mile distant, obscured by a stand of trees—but their isolation seemed complete. They found a few berries and then Nancy put out a blanket over a bare patch of ground by the tumbledown hut, and they sat there watching the river run with their backs against the sun-warmed wood. A breeze had come up . . . the twilight breeze, Nancy called it.

She held his hand, and her skin was warm and dry.

She said after a time, "You like that place? The Burack place?"

Travis shrugged. "It's all right."

"You don't sound too enthusiastic."

"I don't have much choice. It's a place to live."

"You make money down at the plant?"

"Some."

She smiled knowingly. "I bet that Creath Burack siphons off most of it for rent. Am I right?"

"He takes a share. I save a little." She was leading up to something, Travis thought.

"How about that girl upstairs?"

"Anna?" He shrugged uncomfortably. "I don't see much of her."

"She's a big mystery, you know. Everybody talked about her for a while. Still do sometimes."

"Really? She's so quiet—"

"Travis, that's a major crime in *itself*. But there's more to it. There must be. Sure, she's quiet. Nobody knows where she comes from or how she happened to end up in Haute Montagne. One day she was living at the Buracks', that's all anybody knows. But there are rumors. Man named Grant Bevis, used to live next door to your aunt and uncle, married man—he left town real quick not too long after Anna Blaise moved in. Anna takes in sewing but she never shows her face in town. Answers the door sometimes . . . probably gets all her work that way: people take her sewing just so they can get a glance at her." Nancy gazed up at a solitary cloud. "They say she's beautiful."

"Haven't you seen her?"

"Maybe I have. Maybe I haven't. Do you think she's beautiful?"

"Yes," Travis said.

"You talk to her much?"

"She comes down to dinner. Creath does most of the talking." He stretched out on the blanket. "I went up one time and offered to help her with the sewing. She said no, she was fine."

In fact he had stayed a little longer, trying to make small talk. Anna Blaise had sat on the bed, smiling encouragingly but answering in monosyllables. In a modest blouse and skirt she had looked more than attractive, she had been almost devastatingly beautiful, lithe and pale and still, like a piece of china statuary . . . and Travis had made himself leave the room because if he did not he would have been beside her on the bed, kissing her. He felt sure she would not have objected. He could have done anything he wanted. She did not, after all, object to Creath's attentions.

And he could not help thinking: *why, why?* How could she have compromised herself that way, and why did she seem in spite of it so pure?

A mystery, Nancy had said. Yes.

But he could tell her none of this.

"You like her," Nancy said.

He pressed her hand. "I like you."

She said airily, "I don't believe in monogamous love. Does that shock you, Travis? I believe it's possible to love more than one person. Even sexually. I believe—"

He touched her cheek and kissed her.

She moved her body closer to his.

They kissed until the sun was gone and the darkness had closed down around them. He was stroking her then, memorizing the feel of her body beneath the cotton dress, and it might have gone farther, might have reached a consummation Travis had only dared dream about . . . but she sat up suddenly, her wide eyes luminous in the last of the daylight, and said: "Travis! There's somebody here!"

"You want a *ride*, Nancy?"

It was Greg Morrow. Nancy was able to make out his silhouette against the sky. He was big, his arms were prickled with black hairs, his angular face was a shadow. He hunched forward threateningly. And there was another shape looming behind him, one of Greg's buddies, an illiterate millworker named Kluger.

Next to her, Travis climbed very slowly to his feet. Nancy's stomach was leaden with fear for him.

Nevertheless she said, "No, thank you, Greg, I would not like a ride. You shouldn't have followed me."

Greg came closer, his hips thrust forward, his hands loose at his sides.

"Just curious," he said. "Just wanted to know what Miss Too-Good-For-Me is up to. Miss Royal Twat." He spat at Travis's feet. "Rolling in the dirt with a shit-heel farmboy. Well, well."

She stood up. A moment ago, she thought dazedly, everything had been so nice. . . . "Go away, Greg."

"No," he said. It was a hostile, insinuating whisper: "I want you to ride with me."

Travis started forward. But Greg was quick, Greg was terribly quick, and she saw his fist fly out like a piston and heard it connect with Travis's face.

Travis reeled back. She looked up at him and saw a ring of blood around his mouth. He was sagging against the timbers of the shack. His eyes were closed.

"Son of a *bitch*," she said.

Greg laughed. "You dirty-mouthed cunt," he said triumphantly. "Come on, cunt." And his friend moved closer, too.

Greg reached out for her. She drew back against the wall of the shack, next to Travis. Her heart was beating wildly, she could hardly see for the tears that had started in her eyes. But I will fight, she thought. He will not have me without a fight.

Greg came forward again, his hand suddenly clenched on her wrist . . . and then, so quickly that she did not understand at first what had happened, Travis's fist clubbed down on the side of Greg's head, his foot came up between the legs of Greg's greasy denims.

It was clumsy, Nancy thought, but terribly effective. Greg stumbled back and then fell to the ground, clutching himself, shouting "Fuck! Fuck!

Fuck!" —so loudly that Nancy thought the whole town might hear.

Travis turned to face Kluger . . . but Kluger, his mouth an astonished O, only stumbled back and pulled Greg to his feet.

She looked at Travis and thought: *How often has he had to do this?*

His eyes were dilated, vacant. He stared at Greg and Kluger. Greg, crimson-faced, drew himself up as if he might be willing to stay and fight it out; but Kluger whispered something in his ear and Greg nodded and backed off. It was over as quickly as that. Greg shouted once from the darkness, an insult or a threat—Nancy could not make out the words—and then there was the sound of Greg's Model T ratcheting down a side road toward The Spur.

"They're gone," she breathed.

She felt Travis relax next to her.

"You're hurt," she said. "Let me help. Travis?" She took his hand. "Please."

She led him across the dark field, down the shallow bank of the Fresnel to a quiet place she knew where pussy willows had grown up. The river had retreated in the dry season but she took his hand and guided him across a pair of broad, flat rocks until they stood surrounded by running water. "Kneel down," she said.

He went down on his haunches at the edge of the rock.

She cupped fresh water from the Fresnel and washed his mouth with it. There seemed to be no loose teeth. That was good.

His blood ran into her hand and she dried him with the hem of her skirt. She did what she could, then sat cross-legged on the rock with his head in her lap. He was breathing more easily now. The first stars were coming out.

"This is what it means," he said thickly.

She looked at him, frowning. "Travis?"

He said, "You let him screw you?"

It was a vulgar question but she answered seriously. "No. He wanted to. I wouldn't. That's why he's mad at me."

Travis nodded, seemed to mull over the information.

"This is what it means," he said finally. "Being a 'misfit'."

"Oh," she said.

"It's not fun."

She said, "They're gone now, Travis."

"Sometimes you win. Mostly they win. There's *more* of them."

She rocked him. She put her hand on his forehead. "Dear God. This isn't new to you, is it?"

"No," he said.

"What *were* you?" She stroked his hair. "What could you possibly have done?"

He said nothing.

She said, "Was it something about your mother?"

She thought at first he wouldn't answer. But then, softly, he said, "Everyone knew." He drew a breath. "I guess I was the *last* to know. Isn't that strange? That I should be so close to her and not know—not even *suspect?*"

He sat up and faced the darkness. She had to strain against the noise of the river to hear him.

"We had no money. I knew that. We had loans out on the property. Every year a little deeper in debt. I knew that, too. But the other thing. . . ." He took Nancy's hand, and his grip was frighteningly tight. "I thought they were *friends,* her *men friends* she called them, and sure they stayed sometimes—stayed the night even—but I didn't know—I was only a kid—I didn't know they *paid. . . .*"

And then she was holding him, because he could not contain his weeping, and a chill had crept up from the river.

Chapter Four

Travis thought often of Nancy Wilcox. But his thoughts returned almost as often to Anna Blaise, to what Nancy called "the mystery."

Creath let him borrow the Model A for an evening (after he'd promised to bring it back with the tank full—it was three-quarters empty when he'd climbed in) and he picked up Nancy at the Times Square. They drove far beyond the town, driving for the sake of putting miles in back of them, Nancy watching with a kind of rapt eagerness as the road unfolded. "Like flying," she said. "I wish we could just keep going forever."

September was already a week old. The wind that carried back her hair was cool and fragrant. When they were thirty or forty miles out of Haute Montagne, Travis pulled over and parked them under a stand of bur oaks. There was no other traffic on the road and the stars seemed immensely bright. They had escaped the aura of the town; it was easier to breathe here, Travis thought.

"See much of Anna?" Nancy asked.

He had expected the question. She had taken an interest almost as intense as Travis's own. *She's one of us,* Nancy had said the week before, *whether she knows it or not. An outcast. It's like the three of us are connected somehow.*

"The usual," Travis said.

She nodded. "I'd like to meet her sometime."

"I don't know if I can arrange that."

"You don't think she'd come? Or don't you want to ask?"

"I don't think Creath would let her."

"How do you mean?"

He hesitated. But then he thought: well, why *not* tell her? He had come to trust Nancy a damn sight more than he trusted Creath or his Aunt Liza. If he owed his loyalty to anyone, he thought, it was to her.

"It's Creath. He uses her. And I think he's scared somebody might find out."

He explained about the late-night visits up the stairs.

Nancy was wide-eyed, then thoughtful. She put her hands behind her head and gazed up at the canopy of oaks. "The princess in the tower," she said faintly. "She's a prisoner."

"She doesn't give him any argument."

"Doesn't matter. Maybe he's blackmailing her. Maybe he threatens her." She shook her head. "Jesus! I never did *like* the man. But this—!"

"We still don't know why she's there. Where she came from."

"Find out," Nancy said. Her features were suffused with new purpose. Her eyes seemed to shine in the dark. "She's a prisoner. We know that much. And—you know what else, Travis? Maybe we can *rescue* her."

He came home late, parked the car carefully, went upstairs and fell at once into a dazed half-sleep. The footsteps brought him awake again.

It was a Friday night—Saturday morning, he guessed—deep in the hinterland between midnight and dawn. Travis came awake groggily. He felt the house sighing and shifting, the wind talking in the chimney flues. It was a few days into September;

the days were as hot and dry as ever but now the nights brought some small measure of relief, moon-cooled winds blowing in across the grasslands. He pulled the sheet more tightly around his shoulders and drew a deep, shuddering breath. Sleep was only a heartbeat away. But the footsteps came again and they were just beyond his door.

Creath, he thought miserably, and was over-come for a moment with an unbearable sense of op-pression. It was late and dark and he felt sapped, powerless. But wait, he thought. The footsteps con-tinued. They were light, delicate, almost inaudible. He would not have heard if they had not hesitated in their rhythm directly outside his door.

Not Creath's footsteps. Anna's, then. And they were headed *down* the stairs.

He sat up slowly. The sheet fell away.

Long moments passed. Then he heard the front door latch rasp open, the screen door yawn and sub-side.

His room was dark. Naked, he went to the win-dow and raised the sash an inch.

Anna Blaise appeared on the front walk.

She was dressed in a summer blouse and skirt. His first thought was: *she must be cold*. The wind tousled her hair. Her eyes, shadowed, seemed to give back the obscurity of the night sky. She hesitated a moment at the sidewalk, her head turning back and forth with dreamlike fluidity, like a hunting dog, Travis thought, fixing on a scent. Briefly, she looked up at the window. Her gaze held there a moment, though it was not possible that she could have seen him. Travis did not breathe. Then, slowly, slowly, she began to move westward along DeVille into the black shadows of the box elders.

He hesitated only a moment. He threw on his pants, laced his shoes, buttoned a rough cotton workshirt. He was as gentle as he could be moving down the stairs, but he was heavier and clumsier than Anna and in his haste some noise was un-

avoidable. On the dark landing he jammed his knee
into a newel post and suppressed a curse.

"*Travis?*"

His Aunt Liza's voice whipcracked into the silence.

"Travis, is that *you?*"

He froze.

He hadn't made it past her bedroom.

She took him down into the front parlor. It was dark,
but she ignored the light switches. In her nightgown
and robe, Travis thought, his aunt resembled something amphibian, crudely draped, caught in the
midst of some unspeakable transformation. Her
double chin spilled over a lacy collar, her teeth were
in a glass upstairs, her expression was vacant. Christ
God, Travis thought, I have to *leave* this place—
Anna—!

But his aunt said, "She is not for you, you know,
Travis," with a calm equanimity that made him
wonder if she could read his thoughts.

"No," she went on before he could answer.
"There is no need to explain. I know what goes on in
a man's mind where that woman is concerned." She
sighed. She had settled into Creath's easy chair, her
head cocked in an attitude of icy, bottomless cynicism. The mantle clock ticked out seconds as she
regarded him. "You're not the only one. Did you
know that? Oh, yes. There was that Grant Bevis. A
married man, a respectable man, owned the hardware store over on Beaumont. He used to come
sneaking around here—sneaking after Anna. Wife
left him. Took the kids. Still he came." She smiled
humorlessly. "Left town when I threatened to expose him before the church. His letters to her still
come in the mail, though. All different postmarks.
All the same. "His 'undying love'. Love! As if *love*
entered into it!" Her smile faded. "And of course
there is Creath. I guess you know. Don't shake your
head! This is a small household. We cannot truly

keep secrets one from another. Maybe Creath believes so. Maybe he has deluded himself into believ-
ing so. But it is impossible. I'm not a heavy sleeper,
Travis. I know when he goes to her. I know. . . ."

"If you know," Travis whispered, "then why—?"

"Why stay with him? Why stay here in this
house?" She laughed suddenly, a shrill bray; Travis
worried that it might wake up Creath and bring him
down here. "Stand on my entitlements, like that
Bevis woman? It got her nowhere, you know. It got
her alone and with children to raise in a world that
does not welcome hungry mouths. Love, says the
vow, and honor, and *obey*. Maybe love goes. Maybe
honor goes, even. But there is that last. I can have
that much of a marriage. I can obey."

She'll be gone now, Travis thought. Gone wherever she is going.

"She can see into him," Liza was saying. "She
thinks to conceal it from me, but I know. I know.
There is something in Creath that is drawn to her.
Something left over from his childhood. Something
stupid and foolish in him." She added, a whisper, "I
know that part of him. There was a time when he
would look at me that way. The way he looks at her.
But that was a long time ago. Years gone, Travis.
Years gone. She has no right."

"Who is she, Aunt Liza?"

"I don't know." She sighed again, remembering,
as if she were not fully awake. Her voice took on a
distant quality. "It was Creath's doing. An odd thing.
He doesn't ever stop for hitchhikers or tramps. We
were driving back from your mother's place . . . that
last time we visited, when it became obvious we
could not visit ever again. It was late, it was after
midnight, and we were on the road coming into
Haute Montagne—there was no traffic—and Creath
was tired of driving. And suddenly there was this
woman. She stood on the sandy margin of the road.
Just stood there. Not thumbing. Not doing anything.
Standing. And—Travis, *she had no clothes on*. Can

you credit that? A naked woman on the verge of the highway, white as a statue in the moonlight?" She clucked. "I thought there must have been an accident. I would have urged Creath to stop . . . but he had already slowed down, he was pulling over before the words were out of my mouth. 'Get a blanket,' he says. 'There's one in the trunk.' I did so. I covered her up. Creath was just staring at her like a man struck blind . . . and she was staring at him. I covered her up with that old woolen blanket and I led her into the car. We—took her home."

She let her breath in and out, a papery sound. Travis had forgotten—almost—about following Anna. He stared at Liza now, her face round and pale in the faint light that filtered through the lace curtains from the street.

"I don't know what it is!" she whispered. "I truly don't! The way she looks, maybe. Something in her eyes. Something in the raw smell of her. She does something to men . . . makes them helpless. They go to her. And she—she—"

"Aunt Liza," Travis said placatingly.

"No!" Her voice was shrill again. "Don't comfort me, Travis Fisher! Don't place yourself above me—or Creath!" She groped her glasses into place. Her eyes were suddenly magnified. "Don't pretend you weren't down here following her, following her wherever she goes these moonlight nights! Some nasty place. You and the Wilcox girl getting along just fine, yes? But here you are. Sniffing after that dirty creature."

The accusation was unfair, Travis thought. But he felt an involuntary rush of guilt nevertheless. His cheeks burned.

"Travis," his aunt said, "listen to me. I grew up with your mother. To me she was always Mary-Jane—my little sister. I lived with her and I watched her go bad. Not as bad as she ended up. But bad inside her. *Bad to the bone*, Mama used to say. Bad like a rotten tooth. She would not do what she was told.

Took a pleasure in contrariness. In her own wicked shamelessness. We warned her about that man who became your father, oh, yes. He is rootless and insincere, Mama told her. Mary-Jane, we said, you must not squander your life on him. But she did. She ran off west. And he left her. Left her gap-toothed from all the times he got drunk . . . left her with you to feed. She could have come home anytime. Could have! But *would* she? No! Not Mary-Jane. Anything but admit defeat."

Travis squirmed on the sofa.

"You have that heritage," Aunt Liza said, her eyes blazing. "You must be aware of it, Travis. Know it, or it'll hurt you. You have your father's blind anger and your mother's stupid passions. Leave that woman alone! She is nothing you know or understand. You don't need her . . . whatever your body might tell you."

He said faintly, "Aunt Liza, I—"

"Go up now." She sank back into the easy chair as if some sustaining energy had been consumed. "Go up and sleep and don't let on to Creath that we talked."

The trail was cold. Anna was gone. He went upstairs, dazed.

He slept almost instantly . . . and was still asleep in that hour before dawn when Anna Blaise crept silently back into the house, cold blue fire playing like sheet lightning about her body.

Friday next he drove Nancy back to the stand of oaks on the highway out of Haute Montagne. The prairie spread out around them, grain fields whispering toward a meager harvest. With the motor of the old Ford off and the shrilling of the locusts all around, they might have been a thousand miles from home.

Tonight was special, Travis thought. He felt a special wildness in Nancy. She would glance at him, glance away, and then her eyes would find him again.

Her eyes, when the contact held, were very blue and very wide.

Travis himself felt victim to a kind of unfocused randiness. Nancy's warmth next to him on the lumpy seat of the Ford stimulated a painful and persistent erection. He wanted her so badly that his knuckles had gone white on the steering wheel.

He guessed it was understandable. He had fallen into the rhythm of his work at the ice plant, and the days passed easily enough—more easily than the nights. Often, though, he would stop what he was doing, shake his head like a man coming out of a dream, and a deep panic would flood him. He imagined himself growing old in Haute Montagne, growing fat and sedately cruel, growing into the shape of Creath Burack like rubber poured into a steel mold. He felt at such times that he must push back at the barriers that confined him—push, or go mad.

He guessed Nancy felt the same way. She had been pushing a long time. There was that bond between them.

He stopped the car and they climbed into the truck bed and made pillows of empty burlap sacks. Travis touched her lightly. She's anxious, too, he thought. She *wants* to touch. Push down the walls. But she lit a cigarette, her hand shaking, and waved the match at the darkness. Her lips trembled as she exhaled. "Tell me about Anna."

He told what there was to tell. For a time even Travis was distracted by it, the memory of Liza and of Anna's nightwalk welling up in him like a cold sea-current.

"Strange," Nancy whispered.

"Passing strange," Travis said

"Obviously," Nancy said, "she needs our help more than ever."

"She hasn't asked for it."

She looked at him from behind the glowing tip of her cigarette. "You think I'm butting in."

"No. . . ."

"You do. Admit it."

"No. Rushing in too fast, maybe. Remember, Nance, we still don't know anything about this girl. She was out on a highway, naked. Creath picked her up. Maybe she wanted it that way. Maybe she likes things the way they are."

Nancy scrunched down in the shadowy pickup bed, drawing herself inward, musing.

"Before I got this diner job," she said, "I would go over with sewing. Mama would send me over. I've seen the girl, Travis. Seen her up close. I've looked her in the eye."

He nodded. "So have I."

"Have you? And you can sit there and suggest maybe she *likes* what she's doing?"

Well, no, he couldn't—not honestly. There was that desperation in Anna Blaise like an underground fire; it was impossible to miss. But he said, "There's more to it than we know."

"Bound to be. That's why we have to *find out*."

"How?"

"Talk to her. Follow her." She exhaled a cloud of smoke, tossed the butt out into the roadway, a small cometary arc. "See where she goes."

She could not have missed the attraction Travis felt toward Anna. Travis was a poor liar. And yet, he thought, she is capable of suggesting this.

Maybe it was her way of testing him. Or, he thought, of testing herself.

He thought of what she had said in the strawberry fields last month: *I believe it's possible to love more than one person. . . .*

"It's chilly these nights," she said suddenly. Far off, the westbound train wailed. Travis pressed up close to her, put his arm around her protectively. Her cotton dress was like silk under his big hand. She turned toward him, and they kissed, and there was something in the urgency of it that made Travis aware that she had decided to go all the way with him tonight.

He touched her small, perfect breasts. After a time his hand worked up under her dress. He was almost feverish with the wanting, and when she laid herself back against the burlap sacks and he entered her it was like an electric shock of pleasure. He climaxed rapidly. Nancy shuddered under him and he realized, distantly amazed, that she must be experiencing some equivalent fulfillment. Gasping, he told her he loved her.

Maybe he did. It was not a lie; she would have recognized a lie. But he was far less certain than he made himself sound.

Doubt had crept into him even as he performed the act. He loved her, at the very least, for what they had done together, but even that was compromised: it had been too easy, he thought, she gave herself too easily. Women ought not to do that. He looked away as she straightened her skirt. What disturbed him, and what he found hard to admit even to himself, was that the face that had flashed in his mind in that moment of climax had been, not Nancy's, but Anna's: her pale china skin; the eyes huge and dark, violated but aloof; her strangely unassailable purity burning in him like fire.

Chapter Five

September crawled on, the cries of the trains acquiring that special autumn melancholy, and at first Liza Burack believed she might have contributed toward the salvation of her sister's son.

If not the salvation of his soul (he refused to go to church with her, claimed his mother would not have approved), then at least his worldly salvation. She had savored the thought, troweling in her backyard garden those long last-of-summer afternoons. *I have helped save him*, she would think, down on her knees among the gladioli and the fragrant black earth. It was a good thought and in those moments she could almost believe it made everything worthwhile . . . her fall from grace with the Baptist Women, her sister's death-in-sin, even Creath's terrible and unacknowledged private weakness. Even that. *I have helped save him*.

But she lay awake now in the postmidnight silence of the bedroom, her eyes like beacon lights, moonlight shining on her oaken dresser and Creath beside her like a dead weight; and when she heard Anna's small footsteps on the landing and then, a few moments after, Travis's—then she knew she had in fact lost.

She started up after him. By God, she thought, he doesn't *understand!* If he understood he would not be chasing after her! If he understood—!

But no. She had told him once. And she had known by his eyes that he *did* understand. This was no normal woman and his feelings for her were not normal feelings.

And yet he had chosen to follow her.

Strange words flashed in her mind.

Witch. Demon. Succubus.

She went to the door of the bedroom, opened it a crack. There went Travis, a black shadow past the stairwell. And there, hear it now, the click and whine of the front door.

Liza Burack sank back into the bed, defeated.

Travis is lost, she thought, the sound of her own thought grown singsong as sleep too long denied crept up from the overheated crevice of the blankets. . . . *Travis is lost, is lost, is lost.* . . .

She dozed dreamlessly, and the nightwind came in her window like a tide.

Talk to her, Nancy had said. Follow her.

It had sounded so simple.

Travis paced down the moon-bathed street, making good on the promise at last, and it seemed much less so.

Anna Blaise moved ahead of him like a shadow, a lithe and graceful dancer in a shadow ballet. For long moments Travis would walk blindly, certain that he had lost her . . . then she would appear again half a block away, gliding through the umbra of a tossing willow.

Travis wore a thick cotton workshirt and a jacket over that, and a jet of autumn air set him shivering. Anna wore only a blouse, a skirt, navy blue go-to-church clothes (though that was something she did not ever do), shadow-colored.

He followed her, a sick excitement rising in him. There was, at this hour, simply no reasonable destination for a woman like Anna. The town was asleep. Travis had overheard talk at the ice plant about a roadhouse called Conklin's out beyond the granaries, that a man could get a discreet drink there after midnight . . . but it was late now even for that, and in any case Anna was headed the wrong way, toward the nearer margin of town, toward the railway tracks.

Far out DeVille Street the blacktop faded to dirt. There were no houses here, no trees but scrub oak, nothing beyond but farmland and prairie grass.

Travis slowed when Anna slowed. She had come to the place where the railway crossed the road, moonlight glinting off the hard arc of the tracks. She stood suddenly still—and Travis dove down, feeling foolish and ashamed, into the high grass in the gully by the road. When he peered ahead through a thicket of buckbrush he was able to see Anna Blaise outlined against the morning stars like a sentinel, her bare arms shining, her head moving left and right in that oddly sensual hunting-dog motion. *Christ God*, Travis thought, *if she sees me—!* But her attention was focused elsewhere.

Her arms were stiff at her sides, her head erect. *Listening*, Travis thought.

He was suddenly aware of the small hairs prickling at the back of his neck. His breath caught in his throat.

Far off in the depths of the night a small-hours freight express sounded its whistle. Westbound, he thought, tracking over the curvature of the earth—it sounded that distant.

Anna Blaise was marble and ice, listening.

Travis felt the day's warmth seeping into him from the dry earth under his belly. Crickets chirruped in the gully all around him. He gazed at Anna and thought: Why, she *reminds* me of somebody.

She reminded him of, of—

—he closed his eyes, fumbling for the memory—

—of his mother.

Deep currents stirred in the prairie grass.

The night obscures her features, he thought. It was that profile that did it: the head held high, a gesture both defiant and somehow hopeless. It made Travis think of his mother in a way he had not thought of her for years. He remembered—so vividly now he could taste it—a night like this, that first chill of autumn cutting through the air, when he was no more than six years old.

He had been in bed, awake when he should not have been. The farmhouse was quiet. The effect however was not of peace but of foreboding, of imminent danger: because Daddy was out late, which meant Daddy was drinking, which meant he could come home any minute full of a sour and implacable hostility.

Travis could not sleep with this turmoil of emotions in him: the relief of his father's absence, the threat of his return. He lay in bed listening to the trees talk outside his window and attempted to recreate in his mind the plot of *Treasure Island*, which Mama had been reading to him that night. He had almost achieved sleep when he heard the front door slam.

That other, quiet, sound might have been Mama's indrawn breath in the bedroom across the hall.

He covered his ears when the shouting began. At the first thump and stifled cry, he buried his head under the pillow.

Mama, he thought, oh, Mama. . . .

And when it was over she came to him.

She did it always. It was her way of saying *It's okay, Mama's okay*, not needing the words or the ugly admissions they might contain.

She sat in the wooden chair by the window with the paper blinds pulled up and out of her way. "How that wind does torment that old tree," she said, not even checking to see if he was asleep; knowing, maybe, that he was not. Her voice was choked with recent weeping, but beneath it there was still that quality Travis associated indelibly with Mama, silk and sighing, a good sound.

Then, just when her voice had begun to comfort him back to sleep: "Oh, Trav, *look!*"

He sat up, squint-eyed, and went to the window.

She held him on the lap of her old print dress, her bony knees under him. The sky beyond the window was vast, clear, wild with stars. The limbs of the willow moved as if in semaphore.

"See, Travis?" Mama said. "Shooting stars!"

He thought at first they were fireflies. But they moved too quickly and too purposefully and they did not flicker. Shooting stars, he thought, sleepy now. Falling stars. Pieces out of the autumn night.

He had fallen asleep thinking of Mama: of the starlight playing on the bruise that lay like a veined map on her cheek; thinking of how when he grew up he would protect her, would not let any harm come to her; and thinking of those two shooting stars, how they had moved across the dark sky, east and west, as if twinned from a common source.

He felt as if her eyes were on him now.

Anna, Travis thought.

He shook his head to clear it and crawled forward a yard or so.

She was gazing directly toward the patch of prairie grass where he lay. Her eyes were unnaturally bright. The westbound freight streamed by behind her, a clangorous black banner.

Weariness came over him again, suddenly. He felt a stirring of alarm, but it was muted.

There's something about her, Travis thought. Something had changed in her. He could see it in the arch of her back, in the way her fists were clenched.

She had shaken off some of that passive helplessness. In her eyes, Travis thought, there was something he had not seen there before: an expectation, possibly a hope.

But the weight of his body was immense. The night air seemed to press him down.

Anna, he thought sleepily. *Anna.* . . .

Her gaze bore into him.

Hc closed his eyes.

When he woke the sun was standing over the eastern horizon. There were dust motes in the raking light and his bones ached with chill. And he was alone.

Chapter Six

He brushed off his shirt and pants and walked back toward town until he could hail a ride. He knew he was late for work. By the position of the sun he was at least an hour overdue. But that didn't matter. Something important had happened the night before. It was mysterious, not altogether clear even in his own mind. He was sure, however, of one thing: that Anna Blaise did in fact need help, and that in some way she had chosen Travis to help her.

The feel of it burned inside him.

He hitched with a jut-boned farmer as far as the south end of town and then walked the remaining quarter mile to the ice plant. His reflection in the dusty windshield of the truck had been wild, his hair askew and blazened with hayseeds, his beard grown out in stubble, his fingernails ringed with black crescents. At the plant he clocked in, threw a little water on his face at the chipped porcelain basin out back, and ran his fingers through his hair. Then he took up his broom and began sweeping the raucous machine shed.

She must not stay at the Buracks', he thought. That much was clear. For whatever reason, she had been tolerating Creath's abuses of her. But that would stop. He could not say he knew these things, but he knew that something had changed in her last night. Maybe Creath would see it, too.

He worked steadily and alone. When the noon whistle blew he realized he didn't have a lunch with him, that he had missed breakfast, too, and that the heat of the day was pouring down like molten glass. He wandered through the gravel lot, back of the loading dock, to the grassy bank of the Fresnel and sat with his arms wrapped around his knees, watching the brown water flow and curl. So, he thought, what about Nancy? Did he love her or didn't he? And what did that imply in this skewed and mysterious new world he had entered?

Love was unfathomable. He did not understand it. Nancy was a concentration of good and bad things, wild impulses and dangerous urges. He *had* loved her, he thought; had loved her, at least, in that reasonless moment when he slaked himself in her body. If you could call that love.

He knew only that there was this different thing he felt with Anna Blaise, an undifferentiated longing that seemed to rise up in him like summer heat, not passion so much as a kind of ache, as if her perfect body were that garden from which the first man had been cast out and to which all men longed to return. It was as powerful as that. "Love" was inadequate, a merely human word.

He stood up and turned back when the whistle blew again. When he reached the plant his uncle was waiting for him.

Creath wore an undershirt that stretched taut over the skin of his belly and he was sweating, the sweat glinting in the long hairs of his arms, his chest. His face was ruddy and there was slow anger in his eyes. He pulled a checked handkerchief out of his back pocket and mopped his face with it.

"You were late," he said.

Travis nodded.

"You were out," Creath said ponderously, "all last night. Your Aunt Liza was worried sick this morning. You appreciate what you've done?"

"It was a mistake," Travis said.

"Come on in here," Creath said, hooking a thumb at his office, a wooden cubicle behind the machine shed. "You come in here, we'll talk about mistakes."

The room inside possessed a single crude window propped open with a yellow-handled gimlet. The heat was intense enough to smell, a stink like the hot-metal stink of a misaligned gear in the refrigeration machinery. Creath had decorated the walls with calendars: bank calendars, hardware store calendars, feed store calendars, none of them current. The ice plant keys hung on a big ring hooked over a nail next to the door; under them was the truck's ignition key. Creath sank into the wooden office-chair behind the cheap desk, easing back against its protesting springs, fixing a long stare on Travis. Travis felt a wave of dizzy claustrophobia sweep through him. Because he hadn't eaten, he supposed . . . but he felt like he'd walked into a hot sealed box.

"We brought you to this town," Creath said.

Travis nodded, squinting.

"We paid your way. It that not correct? *Answer me.*"

"Yessir."

"We took you in."

"Yessir."

"Fed you."

"Yessir."

"I employ you at this ice plant. Is that not right, Travis?"

"Sir."

"And now? What have you done?"

Travis closed his eyes. "Come in late."

"*Come in late!* More than that, I believe."

"Sir?"

The older man sighed. "Travis, don't bullshit me. I will not be bullshitted. We took you in, and we fed you, and I employed you . . . and you were out last night, correct me if I'm wrong, chasing after our other roomer."

Travis said nothing.

"How do you think that makes me *feel*, Travis? That you would do a thing like that? Act filthy like that while you're living under my roof?"

Hypocrite, Travis thought. You goddamned hypocrite.

Creath waved his hands placatingly. "Now, I understand how it must have been for you. You did not have a normal home. Your mother—"

"My mother doesn't come into this."

It was a mistake, he realized immediately. But he could not make himself be quiet. Not in this box.

Creath performed a patient smile. "Don't take that tone with me. I *knew* your mother, you little peckerwood."

Keep still, Travis thought desperately. He focused his eyes on a 1929 calendar, picture of a little girl, gingham dress, field of daisies. The sky in the picture was a deep and impossible Kodak blue, almost turquoise.

"Travis?" Creath grinned broadly. "She was a whore, Travis."

So many daisies.

"You understand what I'm saying? She fucked for money, Travis."

You could get lost in that blue.

"She fucked strangers for money, Travis, and I know about it, and Liza knows about it, and the Baptist Women know about it, and I guess by this time just about every dumb shit in *town* knows about it. You hear me, Travis? She—"

"Shut your mouth." He couldn't help it. His head was spinning.

Creath stood up, and his grin widened into something truly awful, a jack-o'-lantern smirk of triumph. "No, you poor ignorant whoreson, *you* shut *your* mouth, how about that?"

Travis raised his foot and kicked the old pine-board desk so that it racked backward across the floor.

Creath fell forward, flailing into a stack of yellow invoices. Travis watched a moment as his uncle struggled up, cursing; then he turned, restraining a rage that ran in him like blood; he yanked open the door. His hand rested momentarily on the lower of the two keyrings, the one on which Creath carried the key to the truck.

Well, why not? He had lost his job, had probably lost his room at the Buracks'—had lost all there was to lose in this town.

His fist curled around the keyring.

He left his uncle grunting in the heat.

Nancy Wilcox knew as soon as Travis came through the door that something was terribly wrong. It was the afternoon, for one thing, that lull between lunch and dinner when the grill was allowed to cool and at least a little breath of wind stirred the tepid air of the diner. Travis should have been at work. He should not have been driving his uncle's black Ford pickup, parked now on a crazy diagonal outside. And if that were not enough, she could tell there'd been trouble just from the look of him: his hair ratty and tangled, his eyes squeezed shut as if against some unbearable vision.

She surprised herself by thinking, *Now it begins*. She had sensed in Travis even that first day in July a tremor of wild energy, pent up, volatile as a blasting cap. And maybe that was what had drawn her to him, that wildness. He was like a freight train carrying her down some dangerous track and away from her childhood. *Now it begins*.

She untied her apron—her fingers trembled—and said, "Travis?"

"Come and talk," he said. "I need to talk to somebody."

She nodded and put the apron on a stool. The only customer, an unemployed bank clerk spooning mechanically at a bowl of Campbell's soup, gazed at her in mute incomprehension.

"Back by dinner, Mr. O'Neill!" she called out, and moved to leave before O'Neill, the owner, could stir himself from the kitchen. Maybe she would lose her job. Probably she would. But that was part of it. She would shed all that: job, town, her mother, respectability. Become some new thing. The bell tinkled behind her as she eased the door closed.

They drove down The Spur toward the railway tracks.

"I followed her last night," Travis said. Far out this old dirt road he pulled over. The tracks lay baking in the Indian-summer heat, oily and bright. His voice was hoarse. "Followed her up here."

Nancy nodded. "What happened?"

"*I don't know.*" He frowned and shook his head as if there were some dream there he could not dislodge. "She watched a train go by. I fell asleep. I guess that's all that really happened. But it seemed like—" He looked pleadingly at her. "Like she *talked* to me. Said that something big was on the way, and she was at the center of it, and she needed my help. And in a way it was like I said yes, gave her my promise. Ah, Jesus. I don't know how to say it—"

"I understand." Hadn't she had the same feeling herself? Sensed it, perhaps, the first time she saw Anna Blaise standing huge-eyed in the doorway of the Buracks' shuttered house? Nothing specific; nothing as intense as what Travis had experienced; but that feeling of the woman's helplessness, unmistakably, of coiled mysteries waiting to be unsprung. "I said so all along."

"I lost my job at the plant. Had a fight with Creath. Likely be kicked out of the house, too." He looked at her. "I should go to her while I still can."

She could not mistake the implication in that.

"You love her?"

"Nancy . . . I can't say."

"You love me?"

He gazed at the bright slash of the railway tracks cutting the horizon.

Even this was not as painful as she might have expected. She believed in free love, yes, love given freely and perhaps as freely taken away. But it was not that: the thing was, curiously, she *did* understand it . . . understood, at least, that what had drawn Travis to Anna Blaise was not sex or love in any ordinary sense, was not something she could hope to compete with.

She loved Travis. She had admitted that to herself weeks ago. But he was more than that: he was her freight train, she thought grimly, the vehicle of her destiny. There was little enough in him of pleasure or of happiness; she had learned that. But for better or worse she was bound to him. She had to hang on.

"So how do we help her?"

He looked giddy with gratitude.

"Talk to her," he said. "We talk to her."

Now, Nancy thought. *Now it begins.*

He started the engine.

"Travis!" Aunt Liza exclaimed. "Thank God you're safe!"

She stood in the dim light of the parlor, dusting, wearing an old housecoat, her hair pinned up. Travis regarded her with a mixture of wariness and compassion.

"We're going up to see Anna, Aunt Liza." He felt Nancy clutch his hand.

"Travis?" She frowned. "Why aren't you at work? Are you ill?"

"We can talk later, Aunt Liza."

Her expression hardened. "It's that thing upstairs, isn't it? That female thing." She blinked. *"You stay away from her."*

"Later, Aunt Liza." They moved past her and up the stairs, and Travis wondered briefly whether he might not be insane—whether he had allowed an hallucination to drive him to this extremity. He squeezed Nancy's hand and pushed through the door to the attic room.

He thought at first it was empty. The single brass bed was carefully made-up, the rose-patterned bedspread folded at the foot of it. The window shades were down; the yellow light swam with dust motes. Anna, he saw then, was sitting primly in one corner, in a straight-backed cane chair, her hands folded in her lap. She looked up at Travis and then at Nancy. Her face was expressionless; when she spoke the words were precise and clipped. "Close the door."

Mute, Travis obeyed.

Anna drew in a deep breath, sighed.

"Help me," she said. "I need your help." Gazing at Nancy: "Both of you."

Nancy stepped forward—bravely, Travis thought; though surely there was nothing here to be frightened of?

"You're sick," Nancy said, "is that it?"

"That's one way of thinking of it. Though not exactly correct." Anna tilted her head. "I can't explain everything at once. I'm sorry."

Travis nodded. He was transfixed once more by the perfection of her. Her skin was terribly pale but seemed almost luminous—smooth as jade, alabaster-white. Even her smallest motions were fluid and deliberate. She stood in wild contrast to the barren room, the black Singer sewing machine hunched over the floorboards like an insect.

He hated himself for the thought, but next to her Nancy was gross, plain, thickly ordinary.

"All I need," Anna Blaise went on, "is time. I'm not certain how much. A few weeks . . . a month, maybe. I need time and I need privacy. It's not precisely an illness, but I'll be helpless. And I'll change.

I apologize for not being more exact." She stood up. "If I stay here I could be in danger. You understand? That's why I need your help. The Buracks—"

"I know," Travis said.

He told her about his fight with Creath, about losing his job.

"Then we have very little time," Anna said. "Is there somewhere I can go?"

"The shack," Nancy said. "The old switchman's shack out by the railroad. Travis? We could fix it up for her. If it's only for a couple of weeks, I mean, while the weather's warm."

"It's private?" Anna asked.

"It's that, yes."

"Then it will do. Travis, can you take me there?"

"Now?"

"Now would be best. While I'm still in control."

The implications of that disturbed him, but she seemed very sure of herself, so he said, yes, the truck was just outside; but then the front door slammed, an echo that resounded through the old house. Creath was home.

Chapter Seven

They squared off in the second-story hallway. Creath, obstructing the stairs, wore a deeply aggrieved scowl. He looked at Travis steadily, appraising him. "You have a lot to answer for," he said slowly, "you sorry son of a bitch."

Travis told Nancy to wait for him outside. She shied past Creath, who allowed her to go, all his attention fixed on Travis. Anna was still upstairs, hidden.

"I'm taking her out of here," Travis said.

"You have more gall than I expected," Creath pronounced. "You! What would *you* do with her—pissant farmboy like you?"

"You're using her," Travis said.

"Shut up. Shut your dirty mouth. Your aunt's down these stairs."

Travis felt his own outrage well up. "You think she doesn't *know?* Doesn't know you sneak up here to rape the girl these nights—?"

"Rape!" Creath laughed, his eyes rolling. "Rape, you call it? What are you, her white knight?" He advanced, his fists clenched, his thick arms showing swarms of muscle under the layered fat. Sweat showered off him. "She wants it, boy-o. Don't kid yourself. She wants it, or else why would you be chasing

her all over town these nights? Sure, I've been up
there . . . and maybe Liza knows as much about me
as that Wilcox girl knows about you, you think perhaps? Oh, we are that much the same. The *difference*, boy-o, is that I own this house, and this
house is where she lives, and I decide who's putting
it to her—you understand? *I* decide."

"I'm taking her out of here."

"You poor dumb shit," Creath said, and struck
him.

Travis fell back through the door of the second-
story bathroom. His hand caught on the medicine
cabinet and a shelf of Aunt Liza's specifics came
tumbling out: Cuticura, Bromo Quinine, Winter Pep
cough syrup in an opaque blue bottle. He steadied
himself on the edge of the sink, blind with pain. The
mirror was broken.

He will beat her, Travis thought. If I fail at this
he will beat her, maybe kill her. The instinct that
had drawn Creath to her had turned terribly ugly.
There was nothing protective in it now, only a huge
injured pride and the formless desire to hurt. He
forced himself back into the hallway.

Creath had already started up the steps. Travis
leaped forward and drove his fist into the small of
the man's back.

Creath whirled, enraged. "You cheap little bastard," he began. But then Travis hit him hard in the
mouth, wanting desperately to silence him; hit him
again when the older man dropped his guard and
staggered back, and then again and again, until his
fists seemed to acquire an energy and a rhythm of
their own. Travis made himself stop when he realized that Creath was not even trying to defend himself: he was prostrate on the stairway, his eyes gone
wide with pain and disbelief.

Suddenly ashamed, Travis stood up straight.

"Don't take her," Creath said. It came out a
whisper from his bloodied mouth. "Goddamn you.
Don't take her. She is my—I—"

"Stop," Aunt Liza said.

Travis turned.

She had been watching from behind. There was a terrible, sullen calm in her voice. "You've hurt him enough. Get the girl and get out."

Travis looked down at his own bruised and bloodied fists.

"Aunt Liza—"

"Do it. Do it quickly."

Dazed, he moved up the stairs.

"I hope you rot," Aunt Liza said placidly. "I hope she eats you alive."

They broke the rusted lock on the door of the switchman's shack and helped Anna inside. She seemed already weak, unsteady on her feet. She *is* ill, Travis thought.

The shack was barely erect, weathered sideboards flecked with old red-barn-paint, a sagging tarpaper roof. Inside there was a crude wooden shelf and mouldering mattress, a porcelain bowl and mug, in one corner a pyramid of rust-rimmed tin cans. The unaccustomed sunlight through the open door raised up ancient slumbers of dust. Anna slid down to the mattress. Her eyes were distant and she was panting.

Travis went outside with Nancy.

"We can't keep the truck," Nancy said.

He nodded. "We'll be lucky if he doesn't have us arrested."

"This is just the beginning. We bought ourselves a lot of trouble just now, you know that, Travis?"

"I guess I do."

She shrugged at the switchman's shack. "I suppose I don't look like much—next to her."

"You look fine."

It was a consolation, and she nodded, accepting it. "Well. We need to get that truck back before somebody sees it here. Travis? I can drive it back to the house. Creath doesn't have anything against me."

"You're sure?"

"Yeah."

"And then come back?" He added, "We need to talk. Make plans."

"Sure."

She drove away.

Travis went back to the hovel.

It would take some cleaning up. The corners were black with spider webs. Carpenter ants moved in the wallboards. It was for certain not a good place to bring a sick person . . . but Anna was not sick, exactly, or so she said; and anyway they had no choice. A month, she had said. And then what? What consummation was she waiting for? But he could not force his thoughts that far ahead. The needs of the moment had assumed a dire priority.

He looked at her on the mattress. Her eyes were closed; she might have been asleep. He thought again how delicate she was. Without conscious volition he moved to the side of her, put his hands, gently, on her shoulders. It was the first time he had touched her. Even this trivial intimacy was shockingly intense. Her skin was cool; it was as if he could feel her fragility under his fingers. She stirred but did not open her eyes.

It was strong, he thought, this thing that was special about her—stronger the closer he got to her. Touching her, it seemed as if she had come somehow to embody everything connected with the female sex, was not so much a single woman as an aggregation of femininity, mother and lover, womb and vagina, an exploration and a welcoming home—he blushed at his own thoughts. But it was so. Not merely carnal, as his contact with Nancy had been. There was nothing base in this. The possibility of defilement was not in her. He thought of what Creath had said. *And maybe Liza knows as much about me as that Wilcox girl knows about you, you think perhaps? Oh, we are that much the same.*

Travis could not deny the truth of it. But here, for now, it had ceased to matter. He stroked her perfect cheek, and she trembled.

"Anna?"

Her eyes were still closed. The tremor in her grew stronger.

She twitched in his arms, then convulsed.

Abruptly he was frightened. "Anna? *Anna!*"

She was shaking now, rivers of mysterious energy pouring through her. Her eyes came open suddenly—

And Travis gazed into them.

It was a mistake. In that moment she was not Anna Blaise. She was not even a woman.

Not human.

Her skin felt dusty. Moth-wing skin. Her eyes were huge undifferentiated pupils dilated beyond credibility. He squeezed his eyelids together to shut out the vision, but that only made it worse: on some inner movie screen she was even more acutely visible. He saw her, still somehow Anna, stripped of fat until her bones shone like porcelain through parchment skin, those huge eyes radiating blue fire, rib cage palpitating, fibrous veined wings like rice paper unfolding wetly behind her. And she was watching him, watching.

He thought of the carpenter ants at work in the rotting wood. He thought of termites, beetles, night moths banging against window panes.

He stumbled back from the mattress, revulsion searing through him.

She sat up suddenly—now human again, at least superficially—and stared at him. "Travis! Travis, *I'm sorry—I couldn't help it*—"

He could not speak. He thought of biting into a ripe fruit and finding some foul decay inside. He thought of stepping into a rotten log. He thought—

could not restrain himself from thinking—of his mother vomiting blood into the stained farmhouse toilet bowl, the wages (he had thought then) of sin; of her riding to the doctor when she was almost too weak to survive the journey; of the word "cancer" and of his fear of it as she declined toward death in her stinking bedroom. . . .

. . . and it seemed to him, in that twisted and infinite moment, that he had penetrated to the heart of things: under female softness, this burrowing nightmare; under the veneer of life, death. . . .

. . . and he threw open the door and ran gasping for the air and the clean river water; knowing, despite the way she pleaded from the doorway, that he could not go back there, could not go back in there, no, not ever again.

Interlude:
Bone Finds Work

"Stick with us," Deacon had said, and he repeated it in the days and nights that followed until it became a litany, a kind of prayer. Bone listened, Bone nodded. Deacon and Archie had fed him; they had refrained from stealing his coat when they might have. In these kindnesses they had earned his loyalty.

The mountains were behind them. The land now was flat, often arid, summer-baked. The sky was as huge and tangibly present as the earth, blue or arched with cloud; here earth and sky met on equal terms. The sound of the wind and of the trains seemed embedded always in an immensity of silence.

In each town they were differently received. In one small grain town they were chased a good quarter mile by the yard bulls. In another a brakeman attempted to shake them down for money; they refused to pay and had spent the night hidden in a reefer car. Bone woke up one morning and found that the redball they were riding had drawn to a stop miles from any habitation because, Archie told him, a band of indigent farmers had blocked a trestle to protest grain prices. Fearful of violence, the three of

them crept away from the freight and followed a dirt
road at cross angles to the tracks.

They were in bad financial straits. Deacon had
been bringing in oddments of food or coffee or boot-
leg liquor with his small cache of money; but he had
exhausted the bulk of that and gambled away the
rest in a game of railyard craps two nights before.
"That's all right," Deacon said jovially. "I'm to
money like a sieve is to water. It's okay. You rule
money or money rules you. I'm a free man, by God,
yes I am. We all are. Deacon, Archie, and Bone. Free
men."

Archie said that was fine but where would they
get the withal to eat?

"Money comes," Deacon said. "Even in bad
times. I remember in 1914—"

But Bone just smiled vacantly and looked at the
sky. Deacon "remembered" often and seldom to any
purpose. His talk faded in Bone's mind to a drowsy
hum, as pleasant and as significant as the droning of
the insects. The sky in this checkered land was
powder-blue, cloudless and fathoms deep. Bone
walked, his thoughts extinguished. The time passed.

Now they were far down this road; night was only a
few hours away, and Bone was terribly hungry. Bone
felt the Calling in him, a deep persistent summon-
ing; but he had discovered that he could ignore it for
a time. All these commonplace physical demands—
hunger and pain and the Calling—could be suppressed. For a time.

Deacon pointed out the grain elevator on the
horizon. "Town ahead. Maybe there we get something to eat."

"Huh," Archie said despondently.

Deacon shook his head. "Doubt," he said.
"Doubt and negativism."

"What do you think," Archie said, "they're
gonna throw food at us? Multiply it, maybe—like
the loaves and fishes?"

"You're not so fucking smart," Deacon said. "Just shut up and follow me."

The command was too imperious to disobey. Archie followed Deacon, and Bone followed them both.

It was a meager town. There was a crossroads, a feed wholesaler, a post office next to a coalyard; two side streets of clapboard houses and a scabrous grain elevator silent in the cascading sunlight. The main street was virtually empty. Bone was thankful for that: he disliked drawing attention to himself (the consequences were so often dire) and he had learned to avoid places like this. Had learned to avoid, too, places like the one Deacon seemed to be leading them to, which was the sheriff's office—the jail.

Archie hung back. "I'm hungry," he said, "but I don't know if I'm *that* hungry."

"You can't tell," Deacon said. "Some places like this they run you out of town. Some places put you up a night. Maybe even feed you. I've been fed in jails as often as I've been beat in 'em. Quiet town like this not likely to want us on a vag charge . . . not if we promise to move out in the morning."

Bone only shrugged. It made him nervous when Deacon and Archie argued; the conflicts were difficult to grasp and the anger hung in the still air like a poison. Bone had been beaten in jails, too; jails frightened him. But, like Archie, he acquiesced; when Deacon set his mind to a thing he was as implacable as a force of nature.

Inside the wooden building Deacon spoke to the cop in charge, a small man in a sad brown uniform. "We only want to spend the night," Deacon said. He said it twice, his voice strangely obsequious and cringing. The small man considered them for a time and then nodded wearily and took them to a cell. The cell was tiny, empty, two stacked beds and a wooden bench. A postage-stamp window looked out on the darkening sky. Bone stepped inside reluctantly, fearing the confinement. This was worse than a boxcar, Bone thought; this was like riding the empty ice compartment on a refrigerator car, sleeping on the wire-mesh bottom and praying the hatch-cover wouldn't fall shut. The cop closed the cell door and turned to go. Bone's head swam with claustrophobic fear. Deacon inquired in his cringing voice about food, but the cop only looked at him, shrugged, turned away.

"Well," Deacon said, "it's at least a place to sleep."

Bone spent the night on the floor, shivering. The deep waters of sleep eluded him. He floundered for what seemed an endless time in the shallows, drawn back to awareness by his hunger or by the less specific imperatives of the Calling. He dozed until the rattle of the cell door brought him fully awake. He opened his eyes then, twisting his head out of a pillar of morning sunlight.

The cop stood there and a tall tanned man beside him. The cop was frowning and impatient as Deacon and Archie stirred on their mattresses. The other man betrayed no emotion. Bone sat with his eyes lidded, wary, waiting for Deacon to say something, but it was the cop who spoke first.

"This is Paul Darcy," the cop said. "Owns a farm near here. You want to work for him, you get meals and a place to sleep. If not, you can clear out now."

Deacon blinked down from the top bunk. "Well, that sounds fine." He showed his yellowed teeth. "Doesn't it, Archie? Bone?"

Archie said he guessed so. Bone nodded fractionally.

Paul Darcy nodded in return but did not smile.

Darcy drove them in his rattling pickup truck to the farm, a house and barn and silo, a garden and a collection of outbuildings besieged by wheatfields. They climbed down, and Darcy led them to a long, low structure of two-by-fours and barnboards with bunks and mattresses enough for ten men.

"This'll be where you stay," the farmer said (and his voice, Bone thought, was dry, like an amplification of the rustling of the wheat), "as long as it suits you. We can't pay you but we can feed you."

"That's fine," Deacon said.

"I'll bring something out, then."

Bone sensed that the Darcy man was taciturn but not actively hostile; pleased, if anything, that they had come. Deacon and Archie tested the mattresses and said they preferred them to the jail cell. This was a fine place, Deacon said, "a damn fine place."

Darcy and his wife brought the food: steaming bowls of beef stew, warm bread to sop up the gravy. Bone ate hastily from his lap, watching Mrs. Darcy. She was of a piece with her husband, silently benevolent, her body not large but hardened by work. She gazed at the three men thoughtfully.

The food was good and even Bone's hunger was satisfied for a time. Mrs. Darcy took the bowls and promised them "a decent breakfast in the morning— before work." Bone basked in the glow of his satiation. Deacon and Archie were right, of course; this *was* a good place. Nevertheless he thought: I cannot stay here.

Here I am. Find me.

Bone raised the objection that night, their first night on the Darcy farm. Deacon and Archie were playing cards by the light of an oil lamp. The two men sat on hay bales with a wooden crate between them; Bone lay on a cot with his knees against his chest. "I can't stay here," he said finally, the words hoarse and awkward in his mouth.

Deacon played out his hand and lost, cursing. Then he turned to Bone.

"What's this shit?"

"Deacon, I can't. It comes back. The sickness."

"What sickness?"

Bone shrugged unhappily.

"Sick in the head," Deacon told him. "Sick if you leave this place. This is the best berth we've had." He was silent a moment. Bugs dived about the lamp. "Comfortable," he said. "It has possibilities."

Archie shuffled the cards, shuffled them again.

"Just forget about leaving here," Deacon said. "We don't leave for a while yet."

Bone retreated into the bunk. He was not sure how long he could stay here. A little longer, maybe. If Deacon wanted it. He closed his eyes against the glare of the lamp and listened to the moth-flutter of the playing cards. Inside him, the voice was more intense.

It was July, and the wheat needed taking in.

Bone had never been so close to wheat. It was a new thing to him, strange in its immensity. One day in that long fatiguing first week Paul Darcy stood with him gazing at the wheat that filled the horizon: wheat, he said, was like a child, nine months of cultivation and this terrible laboring at the birth. "It wears you out," Darcy said.

The wheat was as high as Bone's waist. The stalks of it stood up strangely, the scaled wheat-heads dangling at the top like insect husks. The wheat was a golden color, as if it had absorbed some quality of the sunlight, and it spoke to itself in hushed whispers. Bone, like Deacon and Archie, had fallen quickly into the routine of the harvest. They were up before dawn to eat, Mrs. Darcy serving up huge meals of griddle cakes and eggs. Then the work began in earnest. The Darcy farm had been, in past years, prosperous, and Darcy owned two gasoline-powered binders, spidery machines striped blue and ivory beneath their skin of oil and dust. The binders cut the harvest wheat at the ground and compressed the stalks into sheaves; the sheaves were carried up a ramp to a canvas cradle and bound there into bundles. On dry days both machines worked flawlessly, but when the fields were wet, the damp straw eeled into the gears until the gasoline engines screamed in protest. Several of Darcy's neighbors had joined in the harvest and Bone, pausing among these other men, liked to watch the binders dance their slow, gracile dance between the barn and the fallow ground.

The finished bundles were stacked as high as the barn roof next to the thresher, which Darcy called the "groundhog": a long and hideously noisy machine much less pleasant than the binders. The purpose of the thresher was to separate the wheat from the straw, and somewhere in its grinding mechanism of belts and pulleys this task was accomplished: Bone did not know how. The thing was, the groundhog had to be fed; the straw bales needed to be pitched into the thresher. This was a gargantuan task and could not be postponed, and this year there were not the usual hired men because the Darcys could not afford them. Bone and Deacon and Archie and the occasional neighbor did the pitching, feeding the maw of the thresher each day as it roared and coughed out blue clouds of noxious smoke.

Bone worked from breakfast until dusk, pausing only for a huge noon meal of fried chicken Mrs. Darcy would bring out wearily, as depleted from her labors as the men from theirs, and spread on a long pineboard trestle. Deacon and Archie did their share; but Bone, working at his own pace, levering the big pitchfork silently until his hands were raw and his outsized wrists were trembling with exhaustion, did what Paul Darcy said was the work of two men—if not more. Darcy was so grateful that he took Bone and Archie and Deacon into the farmhouse kitchen one evening and fed them at the family table; there was chocolate cake that night to follow the fried chicken.

Over coffee, Darcy asked each of them how they had come to be wandering the countryside.

Deacon spoke of the work he had done in the Chicago Stockyards, how he had been married once and had a child—"but that broke up even before the Crash"—and how riding the boxcars was not a new thing for him. He had hopped his first freight when he'd come back from the war, he said, and had ridden them periodically since. "Now, of course, everybody's doing it." He spoke cheerfully and at length, but Bone saw the way his eyes wandered about the Darcys' farmstead kitchen, lingering thoughtfully on the wooden shelves, the black belly of the coal stove, the rifle suspended on ornate J-hooks against one wall.

Then it was Archie's turn. Archie spoke haltingly of a childhood in Louisiana and his family's unsuccessful migration to New York. Before the hard times he had worked as a delivery driver, cabbie, salesman, "anything that, you know, brings in a little money. Never been married or any of that. Only myself to look out for."

Then Darcy turned to Bone. Sweating under the concerted gaze of the farmer and his wife, Bone said haltingly that he kept to himself, had pretty much always kept to himself, had been riding the trains as long as he could remember. . . .

"But surely," Mrs. Darcy said, "There was something *before* that? I mean, nobody's *born* a tramp—are they?"

Paul Darcy quickly hushed his wife. "Meg, it's none of our business. Bone helped save the harvest. That's what matters."

"But I was," Bone protested. "I was born that way. I was."

He thought about it that night, sleepless in the bunk bed that was too short to contain his outstretched legs and too narrow to support him unless he lay on his side. Where *had* he come from? Everything had an origin. He had learned that. Birds from eggs, leaves from trees, wheat from wheat, spiraling back to an unimaginable infinity. The only exception to this universal law, apparently, was Bone himself. Birds from eggs, he thought, leaves from trees, Bone from—what?

Drifting out of consciousness he dreamed of a place that was not like any place he had ever seen, bright colors and shapes that made only dreamsense, creatures of unbearable wholeness and purity adrift in a jeweled landscape. No such place existed, of course, but the dream of it made him inexplicably sad; he wanted to weep, although he could not.

When he woke he felt soiled, ugly, inadequate. He thought, *I am less than half of what I should be*—and felt the Calling, that sweet high voice inside him, as achingly compulsive as the night cry of a train whistle, more insistent now but quieter, too, now easily buried beneath the quotidian sounds of the machinery, the farm animals, the hot far-traveling wind.

By the end of that week they had finished the last of the threshing; the grain was ready to be trucked to the elevator in town and offered up for what the farmer Darcy said were "foreclosure prices"—twenty-four cents a bushel. The workload had eased and Deacon and Archie spent more time together, playing cards after dark by lantern-light, the sound of Deacon's voice as relentless and oddly comforting as the ticking of a clock. Deacon talked about the Darcys more often. And Archie, often, was sullen and silent.

"They're childless," Deacon said, "and with the harvest over there's nobody within miles of here. The opportunity is perfect."

"No," Archie said. "What you have in mind, that's courting the worst sort of danger."

"In hard times," Deacon said sagely, "taking risks is the only way to get ahead. You want to be a bindlestiff forever? Live out your life in some pasteboard Hoovertown? By God. How else do people *get* rich, if not by taking money from some other person? It's cruel—of course it's cruel—but it's how the world operates, and you can't argue with it; you might as well argue with rocks or water."

"But if we take the money," Archie began without real hope, and Deacon interrupted:

"They have land. They own this spread. We're not hurting them as much by taking it as we are hurting ourselves by leaving it. Darcy could not have made his harvest without us—you heard him say so. We did the work and we deserve payment for it. In a way it *is* our money."

Bone listened with a pained incomprehension. He did not understand about money. The money came from the wheat, somehow, and the wheat was Darcy's, wasn't it? He guessed Deacon knew what he was talking about . . . but there was a bad feeling in the air, the steely odor of Archie's fear and Deacon's imperious needs.

"People have seen us," Archie said. "They know what we look like. We'll get caught."

"Do they?" Deacon said. "Will we?"

"The sheriff who brought us over," Archie said, "the men Darcy had in for the wheat harvest—"

"Look at yourself. Look at me! Think about it. We could be anybody. Any redball freight, there's fifty guys who look just like us."

"But Bone—"

"They see *Bone*. Exactly! Who was at the farm? Well, there was two guys—hoboes—and this *geek*. If they look for anybody, it won't be for us."

Bone understood that Deacon was plotting a theft, that the Darcys would be the victims of it. The idea disturbed him, but he turned on his side and closed his eyes. Whatever was imminent, it could not be helped. He had parceled out his loyalty; he could not retrieve it now.

"But the Darcys," Archie said patiently, "they'll know it wasn't Bone who took the money."

"That," Deacon said softly, "is another problem."

Archie took him aside the next evening at sunset. It had been a hot blue day, the wind stirring dust in the stubbled fields. The denuded earth was like scar tissue. The binders had done all their work, Bone knew; Darcy had cleaned them and oiled them and stored them under tarps, their sleek angles hidden for a season.

"You have to understand about Deacon," Archie said. "The kind of guy he is."

Bone liked Archie. He was fascinated by Archie's wisp of beard and by the way he held Deacon's mirror for him. Now, though, Archie was frowning, and Bone smelled the fear that had in recent days begun to cling to him. They leaned against a rail fence, Archie's eyes furtive in his small face.

"I been with him a long time," Archie said. "He's a decent man. Many a time I wouldn't have eaten but for him. Full of plans, full of schemes. You know that."

Bone said nothing.

"But he's ambitious," Archie said. "I've seen it happen before. It's like shooting craps. The same thing. Get him started and he won't be able to stop."

Archie's hands trembled. Bone perceived the fear that was bottled inside the smaller man. The fear was infectious; it was like a fog, Bone thought, oily and clinging.

"What he wants to do," Archie said, "it scares me. I'm not stupid. It won't end here. I know that. If it starts, Christ knows where it'll stop. You understand?"

But the words came too fast. Bone looked at Archie emptily. The sun had gone behind the farmhouse, shadows lengthened and darkened.

"In a way," Archie said, "I think it started back in California, back during that raid, when you killed those farmers, when you knocked down that scissor-bill like, I don't know, some kind of crazy man, throwing those big goddamn fists around . . . you didn't see his *eyes*, Bone, how they lit up, like for the first time in all his life he saw some guy with a club or a uniform get kayoed. For the first time, understand, it wasn't *him* on the ground, it was the *other guy*, and I think that made him a little crazy, crazy with the wanting of it. . . ." Archie paused, swiping the sweat from his forehead with the back of his hand. "Every time he looks at you, that's what he sees."

"It's not my fault," Bone managed. "It's in him."

"Deep in him. You draw it out."

"Look at me," Bone said. "What do you see?"

Archie gazed at him. Bone felt the smaller man's confusion.

"There's no harm in you," Archie relented, almost tearful now; "I never said that! But, Bone, listen, we have to stop him! If we don't, these people, the Darcys, they won't just get robbed, they might get something worse, they might get hurt—killed, maybe—I mean, I've seen the way he looks at them, the way he looks at this spread, and he's working hard at hating 'em, hating 'em for what they got, hoarding up envy like sour bile inside him—"

But the words fled comprehension. There was only the fear clinging to Archie like a bad smell. Bone wished there was something he could do. But he could not control Deacon.

Deacon looks at me, Bone thought, and what he sees is Deacon: Deacon killing that scissorbill, Deacon with his big fists clenched.

And Archie looks at me, he thought, and sees Archie—Archie trembling, Archie wanting to help, Archie helpless.

He might have said something, might have tried to explain . . . but the smaller man's fear crested like a wave over him, and the words became dim and elusive.

Frightened, Bone turned and fled to the barn.

That night in his bunk he dreamed again of the Jeweled World and woke before the cock's crow, shivering in the darkness. The Calling was plaintive in him and it blended, somehow, into the howl of a distant train. *So close now. So close*

He could not delay any longer.

He stood next to Deacon that morning, soaping himself at the wooden trough. Bone washed clumsily. His naked body was huge and strange, sinews and joints oddly linked, only approximately human. Deacon and Archie had long since ceased to remark on it, but this morning he was painfully aware of his own peculiarity. He longed to know what he meant, what he *was* . . . and knew that the only answer was in the Calling.

"Tonight," he told Deacon. "I leave tonight. I can't stay any longer."

Deacon ceased toweling his face and gave Bone a long thoughtful look.

"All right," he said. "Okay. Tonight it is."

The sky was livid with dawn.

By midmorning an overcast had moved in. The gray clouds hung from horizon to horizon all through that day, thinning but never breaking, and when they were darkest a hard rain came down. Deacon, Archie, and Bone were confined to the hired men's quarters. The gloom was so intense that their lantern did little to penetrate it.

Bone was aware of the silence between Archie and Deacon, the way they moved around each other like nervous cats. There was no poker tonight, no debate. Only the sound of the rain drumming on the sod roof.

Archie stood up impulsively not long before darkness set in for the night. He stretched, shot a glance at Deacon, said, "This fuckin' place!" and ducked through the door in the direction of the outhouse.

Deacon, seated on his bunk, watched the other man go. As soon as Archie was hidden by the rain he stood up.

"I'll be out for a bit," he told Bone. "You stay here. You hear me? Stay put."

"Deacon—"

"*Shut up.*"

Bone recoiled from the force of Deacon's voice.

"Shut up," Deacon whispered fiercely, "and stay put, and that's all I want to hear from you."

Bone sat still.

Deacon moved out into the rain as Archie had, but in a different direction: toward the farmhouse.

Bone was still waiting—gazing at the rain, his knees pulled up, rocking in rhythm with the Calling inside him—when Archie came back, staring at Deacon's empty bunk. "Son of a *bitch*," he said, and turned almost tearfully to Bone. "Where is he? Oh, Christ! Did he go out? Did he go *there?*"

Bone pointed toward the farmhouse—a dark shape in the rain through the door.

Archie staggered as if from a physical blow. He looked suddenly small, Bone thought. Small and old. His grief was like a dark aura. "Oh, Christ, Bone—come on, come with me, we gotta stop him, stop him before it's too late!"

The demand was so heartfelt that Bone did not question it. He ran behind Archie into the rain. He was cold and wet instantly, water slicking his stubble hair, running past the collar of his pea coat into his torn checked shirt and down the knobs of his spine. They reached the farmhouse, and Bone pressed up against a kitchen window. Condensation frosted the glass; he could not see inside; but one wet pane gave him back his own reflection, sunken-eyed, pale, and huge. The kitchen was dark. Archie shouted: "Bone! Bone, the door's locked! Knock it down, for God's sake, he's inside there, *Bone—*"

But then a light flashed twice in the darkness, the noise of it ringing painfully in Bone's eardrums. It was Darcy's big shotgun, Bone guessed. The one that had hung on the wall. And in the eerie silence that followed there was only the drumming of the rain, the rattle of a fallen copper kettle from the kitchen, and the wail of Archie's weeping.

Digging the hole, Bone thought about death.

The darkness was absolute, though the rain had tapered to a drizzle. He worked methodically with the Darcys' broad-bladed shovel, fighting the wet ground and the mulch that littered the wheatfield, turning up the rich dark soil. The night wind on his wet clothes made him tremble, and Bone gritted his teeth and drove the shovel savagely into the resistant earth. He smelled of his work.

Death was not such a bad thing, Bone thought. He had wondered, at times, if it was not in fact death that was Calling him, whether that elusive sweetness might not be the sweetness of release from this misshapen body. In some way it might be . . . but he had been offered death many times and had never accepted. The body resisted. There was an incompleteness about it.

Too, he had seen death often enough among the railway tramps and it was not attractive. There was a kind of shamefulness about a human body after death, Bone thought, the limpness, like a child's costly doll too casually discarded. To Bone, the dead always seemed insulted: subject to indignities, and passively sullen.

Bone had made the hole shallow but wide. It looked less like a grave than like some kind of crater, broadly dish-shaped, now filling with black water. Bone guessed it was good enough and when he stood up and turned toward the farmhouse he saw the halo of Archie's lantern bobbing toward him across the denuded wheatfield. Archie had stopped weeping, but his face was set in a rictus of grief, his eyes heavy-lidded and bruised-looking.

"It'll do," Archie said. He looked at Bone. "Come help me."

They moved back through the darkness to the Darcy farmhouse. A single kitchen lantern was burning, and Bone navigated through a gloom of shadows. "Here," Archie said tonelessly. He put his hands under Paul Darcy's shoulders. Bone took the feet, spreading the legs until he was able to grasp the body under the knees. This was death, all right. Always the same, Bone thought, that rag-doll pout, as if the farmer were holding his breath to protest the injustice of it. Bone looked without curiosity at the broad red stain across Darcy's midsection. They lifted up the body and carried it into the wheatfield, to the hole Bone had gouged there.

The body looked up at them from the hole. Archie, breathing in gasps, poured a spadeful of earth over Darcy's face, as if he could not bear that silent recrimination. There was something prudish in the gesture, and Archie straightened hastily, shaking his head. "One more," he said.

This one was more difficult even for Bone. The Darcy woman lay at the opposite end of the kitchen, spreadeagled next to the iron stove (the stove Deacon had called a "puffin' belly"), and though her wound was similar to her husband's the expression on her face was even more reproachful. Maybe the indignity was worse for a woman: this nasty business of lifting and burying. By the time they reached the grave Archie was weeping again, a dry weeping that seemed to come from deep inside the cavity of his chest. Mrs. Darcy lay in the shallow hole in her yellow print dress, and Bone saw that the rain had made her expression quizzical, as if she were surprised to be here, staring so fixedly up at the night. Bone suppressed an urge to apologize.

"Bury 'em," Archie said. He wiped his hands on his pants. "Bury 'em fast as you can."

Bone drove his shovel into the dirt pile: *chuff.* It was easier work than the digging had been.

Now the bunkroom was full of light. Deacon was there, filling up his kitbag and Archie's with oddments from the Darcy household: forks, spoons, canned food. He did not look cheerful exactly, Bone thought, but there was a feverish redness to his cheeks, a wildness in his eyes.

"A night's work," he was saying. "All in a fucking night's work. Right, Archie? All in a night's work—right?"

"For Christ's sake," Archie pleaded, "shut up about it."

Bone stood in the doorway, waiting.

"We move out tonight," Deacon said. "Find us a train. Moving out, Bone! Find us a train out of here."

Bone nodded. It was all he had really wanted. He gazed at Deacon hefting his kitbag and wondered for the first time whether these men were really his friends, whether the killing of the Darcys had been, as Deacon insisted, "necessary." Deacon feeding him in California, Deacon offering him a smoke— that Deacon had smelled trustworthy and Bone had invested his trust accordingly.

This Deacon—literally twitching with nervous energy, his eyes wild with lantern light—smelled very different. There was an air about him of cordite and revenge. He had killed. He had killed with calculation and without mercy. He could do so again.

Deacon motioned to Bone, and the two of them stepped outside for a moment. "This is just between us," Deacon said, hooking his arm over Bone's stooped shoulder. "Not that I don't trust Archie. Don't get me wrong. He's my buddy. But he's a little wild right now—you understand? I got something I want you to hold onto for me, and maybe don't let Archie know you got it. Understand?"

Bone shrugged.

"Good," Deacon said hastily, "great," and he pushed something into the deep pocket of Bone's blue Navy pea coat.

"Archie!" Deacon yelled. "Time to move out! We want to get down the road before sunup!"

Lingering behind them on the wet road away from the farmhouse, Bone waited until there was a little dawn light and then reached into his pocket and pulled out what Deacon had put there. It was a damp wad of bills, prosaic in his huge calloused hand.

Bone slid the money back into his pocket.

The Calling was louder now, and he listened carefully for the sound of a train.

Chapter Eight

Nancy located Travis on the first chill day of the autumn.

Seasons in Haute Montagne always followed the calendar. Springs were a haste of melting and blossoming; summers declared themselves boldly; autumns hurried toward winters; and winters came down like guillotine blades. She was accustomed to it. The prairie, incising the sky on all horizons, gave up these clinical seasons. But now for the first time Nancy was seriously worried. The adventure was not an adventure any longer. She had lost Travis, and Anna would not tell her why. The cool air and the shedding of the bur oaks seemed full of portents.

She watched the Burack house for a time; for a time she waited with Anna at the switchman's hut. Travis did not come to either place.

If he had not left Haute Montagne altogether, she thought, there was only one place he might be.

She put on a heavy cloth coat and took a hunting knife from the attic chest where the relics of her father's life were stored. She attached the knife to her belt and slipped away from the house. It was an overcast Saturday, and her mother was off at a Baptist Women's meeting. Fallen leaves pursued her until she was beyond the town, and then there was only the dry prairie grass. She followed the southern bank of the Fresnel toward the railway trestle.

She was frightened, though she tried not to admit it to herself. All her life she had heard stories about railway tramps. That they left encoded marks on people's doors. That they stole babies. That they would kill you for the money in your pocket. Sometimes, especially these latter years, she had seen such men come into town looking for work. They had seemed less threatening than sad, worn-out, eroded. They wore helplessness about them like a suit of clothes. The church would occasionally feed them, though Nancy's mother disapproved: "It only encourages them. And the smell!"

Sad. But Nancy did not doubt that they could be dangerous, too. How could such despair not breed anger?

She moved through the empty meadows toward the scabrous iron trestle, burdocks clinging to her skirt. When she saw a faint line of smoke rising up, she reached inside her coat and closed her fingers on the reassuring whalebone handle of the knife.

It was not a big hobo jungle. Haute Montagne was too far from the big cities, too insignificant a stopover, and too chary a society for that. But there were men who lived here, at least briefly. She saw two huts made of tar paper, tin, and old two-by-fours in the darkness under the trestle. A tiny fire burned fitfully. A few men lay strewn on the ground like sacks of trash, asleep, their limbs at random angles. The sound of the river running came back in echoes from the arch of the railway bridge. She moved as far into that shadowy place as she dared.

"Travis?"

Her voice, too, echoed back.

She thought: He is not here.

But then a shadow stirred in the dark pebbly corner where the trestle met the bank, and Travis stepped forth.

She was relieved that he was not like these other men, some of whom had risen up to stare blankly at her; he was, still, better groomed, better dressed. He looked only down on his luck, not broken. It seemed inconceivable that he could have been living like this . . . for days, Nancy thought; almost a week since she had left him alone at the switchman's shack.

"You shouldn't have come here," he said.

He had lost weight. He stood before her like a pillar of stone.

"I need help." His eyes avoided her, and she added, "You left me."

"Not you."

"Anna? You mean Anna?"

"Let's not talk here."

She followed him up the grade of the riverbank, up to the place where the trestle leaped across the water. Travis sat on a concrete abutment, gazing wearily off at the horizon.

"Travis," she said, making herself brave. "I know there's something wrong. I asked Anna about it. She wouldn't explain, but she says it was a mistake—you saw something you shouldn't have seen. You weren't ready." She licked her lips. "It was a *mistake*. Travis, please come back."

He was a long time answering. The wind was brisk, and Nancy hugged her coat around herself.

"Maybe it's true," he said slowly, "what Aunt Liza believes about Anna. She's *not* human." For the first time he looked at her. "You understand that?"

"No! How could she not be human? She—"

"You've been with her. You know."

Well. Of course there was so much she didn't understand. Obviously, what was happening was not normal. Normal people didn't need to be sequestered in ruined buildings for months at a time. But—not human? How could that be?

Travis's fists were clenched.

"I gave it up for her," he said. "I had it in my hand. A life. An ordinary life. She seduced me out of it."

"She's lost, Travis. I talked to her about it. She's just lost, is all. I don't know where she's lost *from*, or how she plans to get back . . . but lost is lost. This town won't help. *We* have to."

She reached for his hand. But he drew it away, and the gesture was so quick and so instinctive that it shocked her. "Don't," he said.

"My God. It's me. It's *me*, isn't it? It's something *I* did."

Travis shook his head no. His eyes, however, were blank.

"I trusted you!"

He turned back toward the bridge.

"Travis! Travis Fisher, you son of a bitch! *I trusted you!*"

The wind tore at her.

He watched from the bridge as Nancy stalked away through the prairie grass. Part of him wanted to follow her. To apologize.

But he could not forget what had happened in the switchman's shack. The thing Anna had become. The experience defied comprehension. He knew only that it was real, and that the Anna-thing was not human, and that she had seduced him into betraying any hope he might have had of a future here in Haute Montagne.

To the west, workmen were erecting a tent for the traveling revival. A clanking and the cry of muted voices came across the prairie. The tent revivals always came to Haute Montagne in the autumn, Nancy had said. It was a signal of impending winter, as unmistakable as the racing of the dark clouds across the sky.

There was nothing left for him but to move on . . . to move on the way these other men did, riding the boxcars and the flatcars. Racing the snow, looking for work. Travis had resigned himself to it.

But not yet, he thought, though he could not explain even to himself why he felt that way: not *just* yet.

He would stay here a while.

Off west, the fluttering banners of the tent revival rose on their guy wires to the gray sky.

He thought: *There is unfinished business here.*

Chapter Nine

Creath Burack, dressing for the tent revival, regarded himself in the bathroom mirror and thought, *she is gone*.

The mirror was cracked where Travis Fisher had broken it in their scuffle. Weeks had passed, but Creath had not been able to summon the energy to make repairs. A sliver of glass, stiletto-shaped, had fallen away from the backing; a black fissure divided his reflection.

She was gone. He could not erase that single terrible thought from his mind.

It should not matter. He had told himself so. If anything, things had improved. Liza was bustling in the bedroom, singing to herself . . . and when had he last heard her sing? A year ago, two, three? And he knew—it was impossible not to know—that it was Anna's absence that had lifted the cloud from her. That was good—wasn't it?

But he thought, *She is gone*.

Sweating, he moved the shaving brush in its cup and methodically lathered his jaw.

Well, he told himself firmly, it *doesn't* matter. None of it matters. Not Anna Blaise and not his humiliation at the hands of Travis Fisher. Flesh is flesh, he thought; she was a woman, she was gone. It happened.

But in some strange way it was not the sex he missed. Pausing, his eyes on his own eyes in the broken mirror, he allowed himself to remember.

With her, everything had been different.

There was a sweetness in her, Creath thought, remembering the touch of her body impossibly smooth against his own. It had made him cry out against his will, sobbing with the sweetness of it. It was a pleasure that cut deep, that stirred him in secret places and made him aware of all the things he had lost. Not just the failing of the ice business or the disappointments of his marriage, but a broader loss: in her arms he felt, too keenly, the narrowing of life itself. You start out, Creath thought, you are a river in full flood; but life meets you with its dams and deadfalls and all its interminable arid places. You lose speed, depth, urgency, desire. You become a trickle in a desert.

He had been borrowing against the wellspring of her, he realized now: stealing back a facsimile of his youth; reveling, in those clumsy bedroom moments, in all the things he might have been and wasn't.

Now there was nothing left in him but the loss. Only that painful awareness.

He loved her. He hated her. He—but it was a thought he suppressed, grinding his teeth together— God forgive him, he wanted her back.

Liza tapped at the door. "Don't want to be late!" she called out.

He had allowed Liza to talk him into driving her to the tent revival. There was not the strength in him to resist her anymore. And, in truth, he was not strongly opposed to the idea. These last few weeks memories had seemed to shake loose like autumn leaves inside him, and one memory that came often was of the revivals he had ridden to as a child in his father's horse-drawn wagon, excited at first by the bustle of it and then, in the hot cavern of the tent, caught up in some itinerant preacher's evocation of the afterlife, intoxicated by the choral voices, until he imagined he could see that golden city glittering in front of him, until it shone in his dreams, benevolent and full of solace. But the solace, like the dreams, faded; and then there had been only real life, grindingly ordinary, powerful and familiar. The dreams were a cheat, and he had taught himself to despise them.

Now, in some essential way alone, he longed for that consolation.

"In a minute," Creath called through the door. "I'm shaving."

"I'll wait in the truck," Liza said.

He made his mind blank, shaved himself thoroughly and rinsed his face, and then turned away from the fractured mirror with an unspeakable sense of relief.

They parked in the meadow and walked to the tent at dusk, Liza beaming and nodding hellos. Tent revivals always made her think of heaven.

Everything was just the way she imagined heaven would be: the glad greetings, the tremor of excitement, the sweet voices raised in song. Lantern light suffused the high spaces of the tent, and the mingled smell of canvas and naphtha rose up like incense. She arranged herself on a bench with Creath beside her in his red-checked coat.

She was still astonished that he had agreed to come. Ordinarily, he displayed a vulgar disdain for spiritual matters. He was religious, she had observed, only among the Rotarians, and that only perfunctorily: the Christ-the-businessman school of doctrine. And even that had lapsed with the demoralization of the ice business. For years Liza had tried to lead him into something deeper, but until now she had not succeeded.

But maybe his presence here was not so shocking. Since the fight with Travis and the departure of Anna Blaise, he had been in many ways a new man. Slower, she thought, yes, as if he had lost his sense of direction. But slower to anger, too, and more humble. The anger was still there, of course, buried in his sullen silences; but with the anger a confusion, an uncertainty.

She was shed of Anna Blaise and was shed, as well, (though this was not a Christian thought) of her sister's boy. And now Creath was with her at a tent revival. Now, she thought, why, now, anything is possible.

The song leader conducted them through "The Old Rugged Cross," leaning on the beats so that the music swayed with a ponderous grace, like a sailing ship moving in a gentle swell. Liza, singing, seemed to rise and spread out. Creath only mumbled the verses, dutiful and uncertain, but Liza rang them out clear and high, each word a tolling bell.

Two benches ahead, Faye Wilcox turned and cast a furtive glance backward. Liza pretended to ignore her, stretching out an *amen* sonorously. Faye looked distracted, she thought, even disheveled. Not to mention jealous.

But that was logical. The Baptist Women's executive committee was holding its elections next week, and for the first time in years, Liza had been nominated for the post of chairwoman. The nomination had been seconded; she had already begun preparing a speech. She was a new woman. Her life had begun again.

The other candidate was Faye Wilcox.

Liza sat with her arm entwined with Creath's. The music faded. Briefly, the only sound was the autumn wind whipping the canvas suspensions. Then the preacher entered: a tall, somber, hawk-faced man bent aggressively at the waist. He gazed at the crowd, a Bible poised in the crook of his left arm, rimless eyeglasses glittering in the lantern light. His theme, the paper handouts said, was "What Have You Done For Jesus Lately?"—and when he spoke his words lashed out like lightning.

Liza let the sermon flow over her. What mattered, she thought, was not the sense of the words but the sound of them, that diving and leaping of aimed syllables, arrows of God. It was the way, when she was a child, she had perceived her father's gruff commands: incomprehensible but so authoritative. The thunder of wisdom. She closed her eyes.

She lost track of time over the course of the sermon. The larger cadences of it were like breaking waves, sin and redemption, heaven and hell, echoed in the sighs and moans of the congregation. Stirring at last, surfeited, she glanced at Creath, expecting to see the animal passivity that had so marked him these recent days. Instead, he was sweating, though the tent was still autumn-cool. His lip and forehead were covered with bright pinpricks of moisture. His eyes were large. Liza felt a stirring of alarm . . . was he ill? The doctor had said something about blood pressure. . . . But there was an unmistakable attentiveness about him, too. He was *listening*. He leaned forward on the bench, intercepting the words with his body. It was the call to salvation, the sermon burning itself out in a fiery rush: "So many of you are enslaved," the preacher shouted, "enslaved to drink, enslaved to lust, enslaved to every sin imaginable to man!"

She saw Creath mumble, "Yes"—and then watched, stunned, as he stood and ambled bearlike down the crowded aisle.

The revival emptied out soon after, the crowd streaming away into the autumn night. Those with cars had parked in the big meadow behind the train station. Liza instructed Creath to meet her at the truck and hurried ahead. She did not want Faye Wilcox to get away unbloodied.

"Faye!"

The Wilcox woman turned, her face constricted and flushed in the torchlight. She held her handbag in a two-fisted grip. Her knuckles were white.

"Liza," she said.

"It was all so fine," Liza said, "don't you think?"

"Yes."

"The choir, the singing—"

"Yes."

"—the sermon—"

"*Yes*. It was fine."

"Creath was very moved."

"I saw him, Liza."

"Well, you must have. But what about Nancy?" The killing blow. "Is she ill? One hears such terrible stories—not that I give them any credence—"

But the Wilcox woman only turned and stalked away.

Liza felt a perverse flourish of pleasure.

Let her go, she thought. It doesn't matter. Let her go.

Anything is possible, Liza thought blissfully.

The switchman's shack was a good quarter mile away, but if she listened closely Nancy could make out the murmur of voices from the tent revival. She reached for the door, and the beat of her pulse drowned out the singing.

"You came," Anna Blaise said.

Nancy sighed, the sound of it closed up in the darkness of the shack. Travis's words echoed through her mind. *Not human*. It made no sense . . . though there was, yes, that indefinable quality about her, a kind of ethereal lightness, a *not-thereness*. And that quality had grown more intense over the last week. She was paler than ever. A strong light, Nancy thought, might shine right through her. "It wasn't easy getting away."

"Your mother?"

"There's a tent revival in town. You know about tent revivals?"

"I've heard."

Her eyes, Nancy thought. The stillness and wideness of them. "I don't know how much longer I can keep this up. She wanted me to go with her. It was important to her. If I don't go it makes her look bad. She begged. And threatened."

"She could hurt you?"

"Not physically. Not anymore. I guess she could kick me out of the house. Might—if it comes to that."

Anna said, her voice softly musical in the darkness of the shack, "I'm sorry to have brought this on you."

"I would have gone with her tonight. But you said it was important."

"It is."

The silence stretched out.

Nancy said, "I saw Travis, too."

"I'm sorry about Travis."

"He asked for an explanation. I couldn't give him one."

"I know."

"He said—" She licked her lips. "He said you weren't human."

"Nancy—?"

"Yes?"

"I'm not."

The shack was very dark indeed. Only a faint beam of moonlight played through the gaps in the wallboards. From far away Nancy heard the sweet massed voices of the revival choir. She said carefully, "I don't understand." Fear had uncoiled like a spring inside her.

"Travis saw too much too soon . . . he didn't understand either. But now you must. I'll need your help tonight."

"I don't know what you mean!"

"Shh." The voice was soothing now. Motherly. Nancy's heart beat in her chest . . . but she stayed. She did not run.

Anna explained. It was like listening to a bedtime story.

"I am," she said, her voice cadenced and singing, "a long, long way from home. . . ."

After dark Travis worked his way along the riverbank to the switchman's shack.

He was not sure what had brought him. A restlessness. An unease. A need to once more *see*—like the tongue's need to probe an aching tooth. The night was cold, and the stars arched overhead in a cruelly vacant sky.

She is a witch. A monster. Not human.

He thought of Creath sneaking up the stairs, seduced by her femaleness.

She was that debased thing his mother had become, he thought, tainted by her sex, but worse, a hundred times worse. . . .

Mama, I'll protect you, said the six-year-old in him.

His head had become a cacophony of voices.

But this one does not need protection, Travis thought.

The door of the shack gaped open then, and Travis hid himself among the fragile ruins of the summer's pussy willows. Two figures in the moonlight. He recognized Nancy at once. The shape leaning against her could only be Anna. But an Anna changed . . . luminous with faint blue fire, which was strange enough, but changed in other ways, too . . . her bones more defined within that frail body, her eyes very wide, her arms elongated.

It was true, then. What he had seen a week ago was not an hallucination. She *was* changing. She was *not* human.

But surely Nancy must be able to see that?

They were squatting at the riverside now, Nancy sponging the Anna-thing's forehead with river water, and where the water touched her skin the feverish blue light seemed to fade. Far off, there was the sound of motors revving as the tent revival ended.

Changing, Travis thought. Though not precisely the way he had expected.

He squinted at the faint figure of Anna at the riverbank, and ancient fears rose up in him.

If this goes on, he thought dazedly, then soon, soon, there would be nothing left of Anna Blaise at all.

Chapter Ten

Nancy was not sure precisely when or how the fear had descended on the town. She knew only that it had come. The *Courier* was full of frightening headlines. Doors were more often locked. She was apt to be scrutinized when she was out after dark. The Depression had deepened; in Idaho the farmers had set up blockades, dairy farmers had spilled their milk into the road rather than sell it for two cents a gallon. In Washington the Bonus Expeditionary Force had been routed by the Army. A murderous contagion was abroad in the land, and Haute Montagne was sealing its borders.

She had never felt more alone.

This is what it means, Travis had told her, and it seemed like infinities ago. *This is what it means to be a misfit.*

Nancy lay on the rosette bedspread in her room. Her mother kept the small house meticulously neat. They were not rich, but her mother's job at the bakery was much envied, and she earned enough to keep them. Until recently, too, there had been Nancy's salary from the Times Square. But that was gone. Mr. O'Neill had not forgiven her for walking out before the dinner rush. Nor had her mother forgiven her for losing the job. It meant a degree of hardship.

Nancy had some money saved back. Listless, she felt under the mattress for the pastille can she kept there and when she found it she thumbed it open. The last of her own cash. A little over seven dollars. Saved for a rainy day. Well, surely that day had come? In fact, it *was* raining, a lackluster rain sliding down the fogged windows. She hated to go out, but she had to.

Anna needed food.

This thing Anna had said was going to happen, Nancy thought—I just wish it would. *Now*. Regardless of the consequences.

She was tired.

When she went downstairs her mother was in the parlor, upright in a cane-backed chair with her feet flat on the carpet. "Surely to God," Faye Wilcox said dully, "you cannot be going out now."

"Have to, Mama."

"Need I ask where? Or why?"

Nancy said, "I thought you had a meeting."

"Damn the meeting," her mother said, and Nancy was shocked. Faye Wilcox did not curse, not ever. Cursing, she had told Nancy, was of the devil.

It occurred to her that maybe she was now the more religious of the two of them, in some strange way: at least, she prayed more often. Clipped, furtive, practical prayers. *Please God, let me get through this*. She believed in Anna Blaise . . . and was that not in itself a kind of religious faith?

"Mama, don't make yourself late."

"There is nothing for me there. Not anymore." She focused a sullen look on Nancy. "You've seen to that."

"Mama, don't."

"Don't tell me what to do! Do I tell you what to do?"

"I don't want to argue."

"I try. God knows. But you have wandered so far. Is it that Fisher boy? They say he's living like filth at the edge of town. Is that where you're going—to wallow in his filth? Or have you gone back to Greg Morrow? *That* foulmouthed trash. A girl is known by the company she keeps. Lie down with pigs and rise up with pigs. If Martin were here—"

"I wish he was," Nancy said.

"Why? So that he could see what you've made of yourself? My God! Are you proud of it?"

In truth, she remembered her father only dimly. A child's memories: the smell of pipe tobacco and the rattle of newspapers. But he had been good, and kind, and he had understood when Nancy recoiled from her mother's absolutism; he had been somebody to go to when she needed to be consoled. She had been almost ten years old the last time she saw him.

"I thank the Lord sometimes," Nancy's mother said, "that he is not alive to see this."

"Mama, stop it. You know he's not dead."

"I know no such thing!" Her mother rose up from her straight-backed chair. She had lost weight these last weeks, though she was still immense; her skin hung in flaccid pockets. "He died, of course he died! Why else . . . why else would he? . . ."

Why else would he leave me? she meant. But in fact he had *not* died. Nancy remembered too well the arguments, her mother's petulant impatience with his drinking, his job, his language: how he had broken at last on the reef of her righteousness; she remembered him saying a secret good-bye to her, hugging her and saying he loved her: "Nancy, girl, this town is too small to contain me." The trains had carried him off.

She had been tear-stricken but proud. This town, yes, this high-collared and corsetted town (which had previously seemed so huge to her): why, yes, of course, no such town could hold him! She should have known. Heart and soul, he was too big for it.

The memory always brought back the tears. She blinked and said, "All right, Mama. He's dead. All right. I know."

"You have to go out?"

"Yes."

"I shall pray for you."

"Yes, Mama."

The money was running out quickly. She stopped by the bakery and calculated whether she ought to buy a loaf of bread to go with the canned goods and the paraffin. Anna did not seem to mind the cold, fortunately, since the switchman's shack afforded scant protection from it. When it rained, the roof leaked in three places.

Susan Farris was behind the counter at the bakery. Nancy stood at the door, uncertain. Susan had been a year ahead of her in high school and it was Susan who had systematically barred her from the company of the popular girls. Susan's hatred for her had been in some way instinctive, seemed to spring from nowhere . . . though it did not help, perhaps, that Susan had already been employed part-time at the bakery under the supervision of Faye Wilcox. Nancy did not imagine that her mother was a particularly kind or forgiving employer.

She turned on her heel. But Susan had caught sight of her and hailed her back. "Well, Nancy." Her lilting voice concealed a knife-edge of sarcasm. Susan's eyes were very blue, her hair blond, her broad Scandinavian mouth scarlet with Tangee lipstick. "You want something today?"

"Loaf of bread," Nancy said. "The day-old."

"Come down to bakery bread, are we? I thought your mother did her own."

"We ran short."

Mechanically, Susan loaded a crusty loaf into a paper bag and rang up the sale on the thick black keys of the cash register. Nancy tendered a dollar bill from her pastille can and took the change from Susan's perfectly manicured hand. She examined the clutch of coins.

"I'm short a dime," she said.

Susan turned back to her, squinting. "What's that?"

"The change. You owe me a dime. You gave me—"

"I gave you change from a dollar, Nancy dear, no more no less. I counted."

Wearily, Nancy extended her hand. "Count again. You must have—"

But Susan knocked her hand away. The change spilled out over the peeling tiles of the bakery floor; a tarnished quarter ran under the display case. Nancy dived after it. "Goddamn you, Susan Farris!"

"Curse me all you want," Susan said loftily. "I would be ashamed if I were you."

"Ashamed—"

"You think nobody knows what you're doing with this food you buy? It's no secret. Greg Morrow told me."

Nancy stood up slowly.

"*What* did Greg Morrow tell you?"

Susan smiled. "That's for me to know and—"

"*This is not a game!*" She was shouting, but she could not restrain herself. She had passed some critical border into a new and strange country. "*It's important!*"

Susan's smile evaporated. "Well, all right! Don't wake up Mr. Lawrence, please! You want to know what Greg Morrow told me? Only the truth, Nancy dear. That you are still carrying on with that farmboy, Travis Fisher. That he's living like a tramp with the other tramps under the railway bridge, and that you bring him food, and that you and him—out there in the mud and the cold—that you, you—"

Nancy nodded curtly. "All right." No need to force that obscenity past Susan's sensitive lips. It was a lie, but not a particularly invidious one; the lie concealed, after all, a far stranger and less comprehensible truth.

Nancy tucked her inadequate coinage back into the tin pastille box. She thought of what Anna Blaise had told her. *A different place. Connected to here, but not here. We have always been among you.* And she suppressed a surge of hysterical laughter. "Anyway," Susan went on, "I did *not* shortchange you," adding, in a paroxysm of petulance: "It was only a lousy dime!"

Nancy took her bread and went to the door. The rain was coming down harder than ever. She tucked the paper bag under her coat. A phrase of her father's reverberated in her mind. She could not recall when he had said it; perhaps he had not, perhaps it was a false memory. But she could hear his voice quite clearly inside her.

Don't love anything too much. They'll take it away from you.

But only if they know, Nancy thought. Only if they know.

Hooded and sopping, she trudged north along The Spur. It had occurred to her to wonder why she was doing this, whether she might be mad to pursue so single-mindedly so strange a thing. She passed a newspaper box and the headline in the *Courier* leaped out at her: HOBO KILLER STRIKES AGAIN. There were dangers involved, yes.

Tim Norbloom passed her in one of the town's two police cars. A block ahead he slowed, and when she was abreast of the car he paced her a while. Nancy counted out forty steps and then stood quite still, teeth clenched, staring through the rain-blurred window. Defying him. Norbloom gazed back at her impassively—warm and dry inside there—and then stepped on the gas.

She understood. A pattern was emerging. The *Courier*, Susan Farris, the police, even her mother: all knitted together. They were the Conestoga wagons, circling, and Nancy had been elected Indian.

Abruptly the sidewalk under her feet was cold, foreign. The storefronts were drab beneath their awnings; the rainwater sang in a minor key in the sewer gratings.

Understanding stabbed like a knife. She thought: *I don't live here anymore.*

At 1:15 P.M. Helena Baxter, the acting chairwoman, called to order the meeting of the Baptist Women of Haute Montagne. This was unorthodox: but Faye Wilcox, who should have held the chair, was unconscionably late—even though it was Speech Day.

Liza Burack permitted herself a brief smile that lingered throughout the reading of the minutes and the tabling of the unfinished business.

The church meeting hall was crowded, though not uncommonly so for Speech Day. Liza had been given a chair on the platform behind the podium and she was able to see the faces of the members. There were twenty-five or thirty women altogether . . . not a startling number; significant, she thought, only when you assigned them names. Haute Montagne was (she had heard Creath use the phrase) a Good Plain Town, and it was ruled by Good Plain People. The Baptist Church was a Good Plain Church, too, and friendly with the Methodists and the Episcopalians, though it was generally acknowledged that the Baptists were a little—well, Plainer.

It was a small elite of businessmen who controlled the town, a city council that constituted also, in large part, the executive committee of the Rotarians; there was Jacob Bingham who owned the hardware store, Bob Clawson the high-school principal, Tim Norbloom of the police department, a handful of lawyers. It had been a clique all but closed to Liza and to Creath, especially since the ice business had fallen on hard times. And Creath's surliness had presented a problem. But now Creath was back on track (though strangely subdued); she envisioned him pursuing a deaconship, which would better his connections.

And there were the Baptist Women. That significant congregation of wives: Phil McDonnel's wife, Bob Clawson's wife, Tim Norbloom's wife: every important wife, in fact, who had not been sequestered by the Methodists or the Episcopalians, all here today, all staring up at the podium. It would be difficult, Liza thought, but here was an important nexus of power; if she and Creath were to climb back to respectability they would have to begin here.

Faye Wilcox did enter at last, toward the end of the business meeting; head bowed, she unfolded a chair at the back. Helena Baxter offered to give over the podium but Faye only shook her head no. Poor Faye. She had neglected to wear a belt, Liza observed; her dress depended from her immense bosom like a sultan's tent.

The business meeting ended. Helena Baxter, somewhat daunted—she was a Faye Wilcox partisan—announced the candidates' speeches. The assembly applauded. Faye Wilcox, as incumbent, was scheduled to speak first.

She trudged to the podium with a visible weariness, and there were whispers of dismay. Liza herself felt a surge of sympathy . . . dear Lord, this was how *she* must have looked, those long years when her husband's indiscretions had sapped so much of her strength and attention. Depleted. Well, she thought. Sympathy is all right. But it was only the natural order of things that was being restored. Faye, after all, was the usurper. Here was her comeuppance.

Her speech was brief and mechanical. She read it from typed pages of Hammermill Bond: "Woman, Helpmate in Troubled Times." It called for a return to traditional virtues. The speech was a morass of pieties without much life or enthusiasm in it, Liza thought, and when Faye climbed down from the platform, the applause was scattered and contained.

Helena Baxter, frowning now, introduced Liza.

Liza took up the recipe cards on which she had written her speech cues and assumed the podium.

There was the sound of rain washing down the high mullioned windows, the musty smell of leather-bound hymnals stored in the next room. How long since she had done this! The thought of it made her a little afraid. She had chosen a stark theme: "Haute Montagne Must Awaken from Its Long Sleep."

She cleared her throat.

"Difficult times," she said, "are upon us."

She let the words simmer a moment in the dusty air of the church.

"There is no doubt about it. Every woman in Haute Montagne must surely be aware of it. A glance at the headlines is enough. Hard times. Murders. Rebellion. Immorality of an indescribable nature. And we are not safe from it. We must not think we are. But the question is: What can we, as women, do?"

She was surprised at how easy it was. She ignored the cards. The words came fluently. All this had been pent up inside her, stifled in a misplaced propriety: she had lived too long in her glass house. Now she alluded freely to the past: "I have seen the effects of loose morality, as many of you know, on my own sister's child, blood of my blood," acknowledging and dismissing it *(Travis is gone away)*; "and I have seen, too, the power of spiritual revival," thinking of Creath at the altar, Creath born again. And she alluded similarly—delicately—to Nancy Wilcox: "Our own sons, our own daughters," the emphasis hardly more than a caress, "are not immune to the spirit of the times," and it was enough, yes; heads nodded; Faye sat pale and unblinking at the back of the hall.

How simple it all was, really.

She finished with her last and boldest proposal: that the Baptist Women of Haute Montagne should petition the city council to impose a twilight curfew "for the protection of our young people." It went over well. She saw Mary Lee Baxter and Beth McDonnel conferring, nodding. Faye Wilcox, she saw, had further embarrassed herself by skulking out of the hall.

She sat down once more at the rear of the podium, and the applause, astonishingly, went on and on. Liza acknowledged it with a smile.

Helena Baxter approached her after the meeting. "I must say, Liza, it was a very dynamic speech. I think everyone was impressed."

"Thank you."

"I want you to know, you have my support when it comes down to voting."

"Really? But I thought—you've been so close to Faye—"

"The times are changing, though, aren't they? You said as much yourself. Hard measures for hard times. I've never had such a sense that we could— well, *influence* things."

Possibly so, Liza thought. Possibly so. And a strange and disturbing thought formed in her mind.

They believe me because they are afraid.

Their fear had become Liza's ally.

Anna was very sick.

Nancy had doubled back along the railway tracks to make sure she was not being followed. The rain dripped through the box elders and enshrouded her as she trudged across the muddy fields to the switchman's shack. How pathetic and inadequate it looked, she thought, huddled against itself in the rain like a cold wet animal.

The packed earth floor inside was dark and wet. The air was thick with the odor of mildew and rotting wood. Anna lay curled on a blanket.

Her clothes were wrinkled and old. Her hair was tangled, though Nancy sometimes tried to comb it out. She was asleep, Nancy saw, shuddering in her sleep like a dog.

Nancy touched her gently and a feeling of the woman's strangeness, faint but distinct, flowed up her arm. Anna's eyes opened and the irises were a profound blue, the color of the sky reflected in a clear, still pond.

"I brought food," Nancy said, hoarse with the wetness in the air. The rain had found its way into the loaf of bakery bread, and she laid that out on a handkerchief. There were canned goods, too, and she had left the porcelain bowl outside to fill with rainwater.

"Thank you," Anna said. She sat up. Her body was emaciated; she was pale and cold. She looked at Nancy. "You've been crying."

"No. . . . A little, maybe."

"It's hard for you."

The commiseration was unnecessary; Nancy shrugged it off. "Anna? Please—how much longer?"

She closed her eyes a moment. *Looking inward*, Nancy thought.

"A week," she said. "Two weeks. I cannot guarantee it."

Nancy sighed.

"You need help," Anna said.

"Yes." She gazed at the not-human woman. "I need Travis."

Anna said nothing.

"You think I'm crazy."

"No. Hardly that." Anna arranged the food in front of her—her fingers long and china-white, but still with that delicacy of motion Nancy thought of as aristocratic. "Travis is simply—difficult."

"You selected him. You *chose* him."

"Yes. He could have understood. He is still capable of it. And I think the best part of him wants to help. But there is a darker side to him, too, and it is very dark and unpleasant indeed. When he saw me in the Change that part of him was stimulated—its fears and denials. Now it controls him." She tore a piece of bread from the loaf. "Old, bad pain in him."

"But if you can touch him—inside—"

"Should I force him to come?" The Anna-thing smiled. "If I could, maybe I would. I can't."

"You *do* make people help you. Even Creath Burack. That time he picked you up."

"It's a kind of camouflage, nothing more or less than that. As significant as a chameleon's ability to change its color. A reflex. Creath Burack gave me shelter because he saw in me some unclaimed part of himself—a dream he had never allowed himself to acknowledge."

"Still," Nancy said, "it was deceitful."

"Not entirely. I paid for what he gave me."

We do, Nancy thought. We do that. She said firmly, "I need Travis."

"You went to him once."

"I'll go again."

Anna shrugged.

Nancy said, "It is *not* futile."

"There'll be a price," Anna said. "A payment. He is at least as lost as I am."

Nancy said softly, "I know."

The railway trestle offered scant protection from the rain. Everything here was wet, the air was wet, the swollen river roared against its banks. Birds had nested in the high iron spans of the bridge.

Nancy found him in the humid arch of stone where the iron struts were rooted. Travis sat there, one knee cocked and a cloth cap pulled down low over his eyes. The structure of the trestle made this a kind of cave. It was wet but relatively private.

She said, "You're still here."

"Nowhere to go," he said, watching her, "except away from the weather. I'll do that soon."

She nodded and wondered how to begin. But he said, "Nancy—what you want from me—I can't—"

"It's the town." The words rushed out of her; if she stopped, she thought, she might cry. "It's the town, Travis, the town is what worries me. You don't know how it is. They're all so scared. Not just bad times, but people are afraid of all the murders going on. And more than that. There's no trust. They suspect me. A police car followed me all along The Spur—just today—a police car! If this goes on—" She shrugged miserably, her coat heavy on her shoulders, her hair wet and matted on her back. "I'm worried about somebody finding Anna. Or else I won't be able to help her and she'll die out there in the cold." Travis was staring at the muddy ground, a constellation of broken glass. She wanted to shake him. "Travis, you understand? She'll *die.*"

"You know what she is."

It was not a question. She said, "Does that matter anymore?"

"Matter!"

"Well, what do *you* think she is? A witch? A demon? Some tent-revival devil?"

That was unwise. He recoiled from her. "You *touched* her, Nance."

"Maybe she's not human—whatever that means. All right. But it doesn't mean she's bad or dangerous."

"You don't understand." He was frowning, lost in reminiscence. "She was so goddamn beautiful! Not just that, either. Fragile. Helpless. She made me want to—to—"

"*Me,*" Nancy said, breaking under the strain of it, crying a little now: "Help *me*, Travis! I don't care what you think about her! Help *me!*"

He sat that same way, one leg crooked, while the rain fell in sheets across the broad boiling water of the river. He had not stopped frowning. "I guess now you know what it's like. It's no fun." After a time he said, "I might help."

Nancy huddled in her coat.

"On one condition."

There will be a price. A payment.

Well, but wasn't there always? It was too much to expect, she thought, that he would help her for some sentimental reason. Obviously he did not love her anymore; all this ordeal had knocked the love right out of him. And out of me, she thought, confessing it to herself: out of me, too. She said, bleakly, "What condition?"

"Tell me." He touched her, his hand hot on her. "Tell me what she is."

After a moment she nodded yes.

Chapter Eleven

Nancy told it the best way she could, shivering in the damp. She wished she could be Anna, could communicate these truths with that same reassuring candor. But she was only herself. She did not look at Travis's eyes; the fear and the cynicism there were too frightening.

Her voice was quavery and small in the silence. Anna, she said carefully, was from another time and place, another world, very far away in one sense, but in another very near; a world that was very ancient but that had always had a tenuous connection with this one . . . and she closed her eyes, and the words echoed in her memory. . . .

"The passage between is freer for us," Anna had said, her eyes wide and her emaciated body very still, "though it can work the other way, too. There is the ancient human tradition of the vision-quest, the spirit-walk. The Greeks at Eleusis, the American Indians in the wilderness, the stylites on their pillars. They all want the same thing. To *see*—if only for a moment. A glimpse of the Jeweled World." And Nancy, listening, had felt a curious kind of recognition, intuitive, as if *she* had seen that place, too, as if it had been vouchsafed to her in some long-forgotten dream. A shining antipodes. She saw it in the darkness. A landscape of perfect shapes.

"Faerie," she said breathlessly. "The land under the hill."

"In a way. But a real place, too. Substantial. The laws of nature function differently there, I think, but they do function, and as remorselessly as here. A place, not a land of abstractions." She sighed, a papery sound. "When we cross—and we have our own vision-quests, our own spirit-walks—we've been called by other names. Demon, succubus, changeling. . . ."

"But you're not that."

"It depends," Anna said, her smile sphinxlike, "on who you ask."

Nancy struggled to shape her thoughts. "But I mean . . . in spite of everything, it doesn't seem as if . . . I mean, you know history and you speak English and you have a name. . . ."

All that, Anna said, was a kind of camouflage. When she'd entered this world she had put on humanity like a suit of clothes . . . but a real humanity, flesh and blood and psyche; there was a physical change. Creath Burack had found her newly minted, days old; lost, but with a functioning human body and a store of human knowledge. "All the teeming voices of humanity are there to delve and borrow. . . ."

"You read minds?"

"In a sense. The minds beneath minds. I can't read your thoughts, if that's what you mean."

"You invented Anna Blaise."

"In a way I made her out of parts. But I *am* Anna Blaise. Anna Blaise is a translation of myself."

"There was Creath. And Grant Bevis. And Travis Fisher."

"Understand," Anna said. She touched Nancy's forehead, and again there was that quaver of strangeness. "In here, you—all of you—are many things at once. Male *and* female. Adult *and* child. Paradoxes upon paradoxes. Whereas we are made more simply. Think of Anna Blaise as the pole of a magnet. Think of the way a magnet works on iron filings—quite without volition."

"Magnets," Nancy said, "have two poles."

"You are," Anna said, "very astute."

Nancy took a cigarette and gave one to Travis, the last of a dearly bought packet of Wings. She trembled, lighting it. The dampness of the air almost smothered the match flame. She allowed herself to look at him as he inhaled a lungful of smoke, held it a moment, released it like steam into the cold. His face was unreadable.

"Lost," Travis said. "You said she's lost?"

And Nancy felt a surge of hope.

Two of them had journeyed here together.

It was not traveling in any sense Nancy would recognize, Anna had said, but she could imagine it that way if she wished: an ocean voyage, say. There had been a storm; in effect the two of them had been shipwrecked. Lost and separated in a huge and quite foreign land. They were essential to one another; separately they were powerless, embedded in their disguises, more human than not. Alone she was powerless even to attempt to leave this place. Together it might be possible . . . but they had lost one another. They were castaways.

She had needed a place to conceal herself. The elementary femaleness of the Anna Blaise persona helped: Creath had secreted her in the boardinghouse like a buried treasure. It had not been pleasant but it had been necessary; the environment in which she found herself, its seasons and its people, was wildly hostile. And, touching her, Nancy found herself imagining it: Anna-made-human lost in the prairie darkness, disoriented, Creath Burack wrapping a blanket around her, pulling her into the car, into the hot miasma of his maleness, the stink of his cigars; Liza Burack gazing on with a disapproval that would mature into a kind of stony, impotent hatred. In all this, her terrible aloneness.

"But this Other," Nancy said. "He's looking for you?"

She nodded.

"Has been—since you moved in with the Buracks?"

"Yes."

"He's like you?"

A frown had crossed her face. "No."

"A man."

"In his human avatar, yes. Nancy, listen: among us male and female mean something very different. Apart, we're very nearly two distinct species. Bone is *not* like me."

"That's his name? Bone?"

"The name he was given. His disguise is poorer and his nature is more elementary. He's been searching, yes, but we've only just made contact. It's easier," she said faintly, "when the need is more profound."

A tramp, drawn by the cigarette smoke, stood staring at Nancy and Travis. She had taken to wearing the whalebone knife as a matter of course and her hand strayed to it now. The tramp's face was a cipher, eyes lidded and expressionless. His hands were buried in his pockets.

"Come on," Travis said.

The rain had tapered off, though the thick gray clouds still tumbled overhead. The prairie was shrouded and wet-smelling, the horizon invisible. They walked a distance along the railway tracks, Travis scuffing up the gravel between the ties. She wondered what was going on in his head. Whether he believed her . . . but he must, she thought; it was no more fanciful than his own intuition; it was Travis, after all, who had insisted that Anna was not human. "Bone," he said abruptly, "what the hell kind of name is that?"

"He's not like her."

"She needs him?"

"She's sick."

"Sick how?"

"Sick with the separation. They were never meant to be apart so long. Their time ran out, and it's hurting her."

We can't sustain ourselves this way, she had said: we can't sustain our humanity. Or be sustained if we lose it. The changes *must* come. . . .

"This Bone: he's sick, too?"

She said, "Yes, but it's not the same kind of sickness. The need is intense in both of them. Bone is different: he doesn't talk much, he has trouble with ideas, maybe doesn't even know for sure where he is or where he came from. Only that he's trying to find her. He's like an animal following an instinct. He's big, he's very strong, but the time is running out for him, too. But he knows where to find her, which direction to go: she thinks he'll be here. Soon."

"Christ God." He shook his head. "Nancy—"

"You saw some of it, didn't you? You saw her Change."

"I don't ever want to see it again."

The afternoon had edged on. The sun was headed down. Nancy felt cold, tired, hungry. Her flat-soled shoes were all scuffed up and there were burdocks clinging to her cloth coat.

"I don't trust her," Travis said, still, gazing back at Haute Montagne where it stood on the prairie, the towers of the granaries stark against the sky. How small it looked from here, Nancy thought. "She could be anything," he said, "you ever think of that? We don't know what she is or what this Bone is. Only what she tells us. And she's lied before."

"I believe her," Nancy said.

"Maybe she picked us because we'd believe her. Not Creath, not Aunt Liza, not anybody else in town."

"Because we'd *understand*." Oh, Travis, she thought, I've touched her, I *know*—but how to explain that? "Out at the tracks that night, she saw something in you, a goodness—"

"Or a gullibility."

"Travis, what is it? Why does she frighten you so?"

He was a long time answering. The answer had sprung up in him but there was no way to articulate it: because of what Mama was, he thought, because of how she died; because of what he had done with Nancy and what he had wanted to do with Anna Blaise. The whole sour mess of it. He felt torn inside: some wound there had been opened. Fundamentally, he distrusted the femaleness of the Anna-thing; like all femaleness it concealed too much.

"It had to be us," Nancy was saying. "She took a chance, you know, telling us anything at all. But she needs somebody. She can't live out these two weeks without somebody to bring her food, somebody to help her through the Changes—somebody who'll know and somebody who'll do it anyway. You know anybody else who'd do that? Anybody else back *there?*"

"It's only a town," Travis said.

"They hate us."

He looked at her. She was skinny and dragged-out looking. Her hair was tangled. "You still believe that? You're too good for them?"

She straightened defiantly and her eyes went shiny with tears. "This town," she said, "this goddamn town—I am *too big* for this town!"

And a look of surprise washed over her.

"That's why she picked us," Travis said gently. "We're alone. Cut off."

"Like she is."

"Maybe." He added, "When wolves go after a sheep, the first thing they do is cut it off from the flock."

"That's just crazy. She's so weak!"

"What about this Bone? What if they do get together?" He thought of his vision of Anna Blaise—wet wings unfolding behind her. "They don't care about us."

"Come tomorrow," Nancy said. "Talk to her." She said, her voice rising, "I told you what you wanted to know!"

"I didn't make any promises."

"Travis, the only goddamn wolves around here are the ones in Haute Montagne, and they *are* circling, and they *have* cut me off—both of us—and, Travis, maybe you can ride away from it all, but—goddammit—I can't, and they're gonna bring me *down!*"

He thought of Anna Blaise in her damp shack, her pale skin stretched fine, her eyes huge and burning; he thought of this Bone, hardly human, tracking her across the night. He closed his eyes. *The Jeweled World.* He trembled, thinking of it: of what she had been and what she might become. And what he stood to lose or gain in the process.

"Tomorrow," Nancy said.

"Maybe," he said softly. "Maybe."

Chapter Twelve

Creath Burack nodded, not cordially, at the sullen-faced boy who had come through the door of his office.

He felt content, alone here in this pineboard room. There was the reassuring rumble of the compressors, the metallic smell of the dust, the calendars tacked on the wall like pieces of mosaic. He had spent much of his life here. He sat in the wooden reclining chair with his feet on an upturned wastebasket. Too long in this position and the narrow bands of the back-support bit into his spine like teeth. He was getting older; comfort, like most things, could be taken only in moderation. He stirred dully, sat up, blinking.

"Heard you might have a job free," the boy said.

Creath Burack squinted.

"You," he said, "you're Greg Morrow, aren't you? Bill Morrow's kid?" He nodded to himself. He remembered Bill Morrow, a fat granary worker who used to show up at the First Baptist stinking of flax and bathtub liquor, sullen little dark-skinned wife who had died of rheumatic fever three years back—yeah. "Yeah, I seen you before. Aren't you working over at the mill?"

"Got laid off," the boy said. "Heard about your job."

My Christ, the older man thought, but he is not handsome. Round ugly face. And his lip curled like that. Creath felt a swelling resentment of the boy's youth, plainly misspent. He could think of no good reason not to show this kid the gate. But play him, first, he thought—like a fish on a line. "What job's that?"

"The one the shit-heel farmboy lost," Greg said, maybe sensing that he was not welcome here.

"Shit-heel farmboy, huh." Creath was secretly amused. "You got a strange idea how to beg for a job."

"Fuck it, I'm not begging," Greg Morrow said. He turned to the door.

Some instinct made Creath say, "Hang on a minute."

Greg hesitated.

"It's not much of a job," Creath said. "Pick up trash, stand in on the machine sometimes, deliver sometimes, lift and load always." He smiled. "It pays shit."

Greg remained sullen but appeared confused, as if he had been praised and scolded both at once. That was good.

"Try it out," Creath said. "See if you can get a handle on it."

"Now?" The kid brightened.

"Right now."

That had been before lunch.

The kid worked straight through, mopping down the loading docks with scalding water and ammonia. Then the work crew filtered back, gazing at Greg with mute curiosity, at the enthusiastic way Creath played foreman to him; slowly they had caught on, finding him scutwork of their own, lolling against the limp boards of the icehouse while Greg Morrow manhandled the big slabs in and out with an inadequate pair of tongs. The muffled laughter became audible, and at one point Greg looked around with a dark, startled suspicion in his eyes. But everyone had turned away.

After the five o'clock bell he showed up back in Creath's office, steaming wet and obviously exhausted. Natural enough, Creath thought. He had done the work of two men.

"What time do I come in tomorrow?"

"Sleep late." Creath grinned at him. "The job's not available."

"What the fuck—"

"We're not hiring. Thanks anyway."

"You bastard, you owe me a day's pay!"

"I don't remember signing anything," Creath said mildly. "And watch your dirty mouth."

Greg did a long slow burn but he did, at last, turn to leave. Creath felt an immense, perverse satisfaction. Damn but hadn't the kid done a job with that mop!

But Greg hesitated and turned back to him now, smiling faintly, and his posture took on that easy insolence again. Creath said, "You too dumb to find the door?"

"Maybe I'm good for something after all."

Creath was instantly suspicious. "I don't get it."

"You want her back?"

"Want who back?"

"You know."

The insinuation was plain.

Creath felt beads of sweat break out on his forehead. Guilt and doubt gusted over him both at once. By God, he thought, I have put all that behind me.

Demons of lust, he thought. Demons of—of—

"I can find her," Greg Morrow said, and he was smiling now, a secret and insinuating smile. "I know where she is. I can find her."

I have put all that behind me.

"I don't want to know," Creath said faintly. "I don't want to know!"

"Maybe you don't. That's okay. I'll get lost." He opened the door.

"No," Creath heard himself say. "Wait. . . ."

"Huh?"

"Be in at nine," Creath said weakly.

Greg Morrow only nodded.

The kid was gone, then, and Creath sat back, swabbing his forehead with his big checked handkerchief. After a moment he took out the bottle of Saskatchewan corn whiskey he kept in the bottom drawer, Volstead Act or no Volstead Act; he drank from the neck of the bottle. Backsliding. But there were worse demons than Demon Drink.

The memory of the tent revival came back blindingly strong—the fine high euphoria that had blossomed like a thorny wildflower behind his eyes. The two ecstasies warred inside him. Ecstasy of sin, ecstasy of faith. He felt his heart falter in his chest.

I know where she is, the boy had said. *I can find her*.

Was it possible? That she was still here, still in Haute Montagne, hidden somewhere—was that truly possible?

No, Creath thought. It's a ruse, a trick, a lie. It cannot be. It must not be allowed.

He reached a second time for the bottle.

God forgive me, he thought. *I want her back*.

His hand was trembling.

Still smarting with humiliation, Greg Morrow nursed the spastic Model T down the south end of The Spur, out past the scabbed towers of the granaries to his daddy's property, with its sprung doors like torn hip pockets and its elephant's graveyard of rust-pocked farm machinery.

Inside, his old man was asleep. Dusk gathered complex shadows about the prostrate form on the sofa in the front room. A bottle of hooch, inevitably, lay on the plank floor next to him.

Greg experienced a wave of disgust. He harbored no illusions about the sort of man his father was. Shit-poor, he thought, shit-drunk—and shit-stupid.

He stomped into the kitchen. There were cans of charity food from the churches, a few, in the cupboard. Hoover, one of his father's five aging and incontinent cats, sat smugly on the wooden countertop. Greg put out his arm and swiped Hoover down to the peeling linoleum.

Shit-stupid, he thought, that was the sum of it. This town had reduced his old man to a kind of ruin, a living analogue of the junk machines rotting in the front yard, and there was no reason for it but a blind, complacent stupidity.

Greg had not done all that well in school and had left, in any case, when he was old enough to work. But he had discovered a simple truth that raised him above the level of his old man.

Small actions, he thought, have big consequences.

You pull strings. That was how it was done. He had watched the people who ran the town, and that was how they did it. Nothing big, nothing showy. A tug here, a tug there.

And more: *Anyone could do it*.

Today, for instance. Maybe he had endured that humiliation at the ice plant. But he had also got himself a job.

And all it took, he thought, was a word. The *right* word.

There were times he wished he could communicate this truth to his father. If they beat on you, he wanted to say, you don't have to beat back, and you don't have to take it (though his father had done both, copiously)—you just have to *watch*. And *know*. And learn the words to say, the strings to pull.

Revenge was available.

In his head Greg had kept a running tabulation of every humiliation he had suffered, every beating he had endured. His own and his old man's. The memories were polished with handling.

He thought of Creath Burack. He thought of Travis Fisher and Nancy Wilcox.

Strings, hc thought. Lots of strings there.

He opened a can of beans and chased Hoover, yowling, out the back door.

Night had begun to fall.

In the darkness under the railway trestle Travis dreamed.

His dreams were not coherent. Delirious with the cold, he was ravaged by visions. He dreamt of the Pale Woman, and recognized her from a lifetime of dreams: she was pure, virginal, white-robed; her face was his mother's face except when it was Anna's or, somehow, Nancy's. He knew from looking at her that she was untouched, utterly female, desirable— and he was ashamed of his own arousal. He wanted to touch her, defile her. And in the dream she was always moving away from him, retreating, unapproachable; her purity, like some fundamental principle, was preserved.

He woke shivering in the darkness as the night freight passed by above him. Sparks showered down and the roaring made his ears ache dully. When the train was gone there was only the sound of the prairie wind rattling in the high beams of the trestle.

He sat up, frightened, the residue of the dream lingering in the dark air. If he closed his eyes he could see her, the Pale Woman, as clearly as ever. She was, he realized, the woman his mother had not been, the woman his mother had failed to be; she was the woman he had looked for in Nancy, too, and most particularly in Anna Blaise.

The woman he had not found.

And he thought, shivering in the darkness, stricken: What if there is no such woman? What if she doesn't exist?

Chapter Thirteen

Nancy spent the next day at the switchman's shack waiting for Travis to arrive, leaping up with a mixed gladness and terror whenever she heard a sound outside.

"He might come," Anna admitted, her white stick-fingers laced in her lap. "If he does, he will have taken a step away from being—" She hesitated. "The thing he might have become."

"He'll be here," Nancy said.

Anna was visible in the band of daylight falling through the open door. No one would mistake her for human now, Nancy thought. The Change had progressed too far. It was, Anna had explained, the natural sloughing-off of her humanity. But her need, the sickness of her separation from Bone, was also visible. The exaggerated orbit of her joints, the wildness of her eyes and the thinness of her lips, had only emphasized her decline. Nancy looked at her and thought of a child's toy, one of those loose-jointed slat puppets connected by bits of string . . . but made of china or porcelain rather than wood, and with bright blue balls of glass for eyes.

"He might," Anna said, "but he might not. You should be prepared for that."

Her plain prairie accent, coming from that body, was like a bad joke. But no, Nancy thought, not really. The voice, for all its plainness, was high and lilted, a kind of song, like singing heard far off on a summer night, and it was that voice, the reassurance of it, that helped keep Nancy sane through all this. Physically Anna was frighteningly strange; she *was* alien, now unmistakably so; but that wonderful half-familiar voice contained a calming cadence, a necessary link to the known.

"He'll come," Nancy said, and: "What do you mean—a step away from being *what?*"

"He's two people. You must have seen that. Part of him is the Travis who has been so often hurt and victimized, and that part of him is sympathetic. He *wants* to help. But there is this other Travis Fisher, the Travis Fisher who believes in a kind of female purity, who believes that women ought to be pristine, above nature, incorruptible—all the things he thought I was."

"Or the things you chose to show him."

"Maybe I deluded him. If so, it was not by choice. It's in my nature to be a mirror. Like Creath, he looked at me and saw a hidden part of himself."

It was at such times, Nancy thought, that Anna seemed most wholly alien. Her eyes grew distant, as if she were looking directly into Travis's skull, peering somehow into the coral growths of his unconscious mind. Nancy had taught herself something about modern psychology; yes, she thought, there is some truth in all this. "He believed in you."

"He thought I was that woman. But he wanted you to be that woman, too. The woman he once believed his mother was."

His mother, Nancy thought, yes, my God. "He must feel—betrayed—"

"Betrayed and angry. And that's the other part of Travis Fisher: this huge anger. A part of him hates us—hates both of us—for not being pure enough or good enough."

"There were times," Nancy said, nodding, "the way he'd look at me—"

"He suppresses the hate, of course. He believes in chivalry. And unlike Creath he is not by nature cruel. But the hate has had a good deal of trauma to feed on. It could displace his better instincts."

"But if he understood—"

"It's not as simple as that. All this lives in the deepest part of him."

"Phantoms," Nancy said scornfully. "Ghosts."

Anna shrugged. "Travis's virtuous woman is a kind of ghost, yes. Like *your* ghost." Nancy frowned. "The ghost," Anna went on, "of your father. Or the man you invented out of the memory of your father. The ghost you've been trying to placate all these years. . . ."

"I thought you couldn't read minds."

"Only the deepest parts." After a moment: "I'm sorry." Her voice was faint. "I shouldn't have spoken."

Nancy was astonished to find her eyes filling with tears. She dabbed her face with the wrists of her blouse. It was all crazy, of course. Anna was *not* human; Travis was right; she could hardly be expected to understand how real people thought or felt. "It's not really like that." She turned back defiantly. "He was—he—"

But Anna held up her hand, pleadingly. "Truly, I'm sorry. I have to rest now."

Nancy went out into the meadow—the sun was disturbingly low in the sky—to wait for Travis. He would come. He must. But the meadow was empty and the wind cut through this threadbare winter coat like a darning needle. She hugged herself and went back to the meager shelter of the switchman's shack. Inside, she let her head loll against the fibrous wallboards and closed her eyes. When she opened them she gasped.

Anna was convulsing.

Her eyes had rolled up into her head. Her skin, always alarmingly pale, was dead-white now, blood-drained. The convulsions traversed her body; her spine bucked and arched over the thin stained mattress. . . .

"Anna!"

This was not the Change, Nancy thought dazedly, this was something else. Something new, something worse. She put her arm around the alien woman to steady her.

The contact was electric. So quickly that she could not steel herself, her mind was filled with hideous images.

The earth lurching under her feet. Fear. Fear and the footsteps behind her. A train roaring blackly in the near distance. The cold wind, the footsteps, the gun, the shockingly loud sound of it, pain invading her body in huge radiant arcs—

—and she was distantly aware of the scream that filled the confined space of the shack: it might have been Anna's, or hers, or both.

Liza Burack picked up the phone on the second ring. She had been answering telephones more eagerly this autumn now that she had come to believe in the possibility of good news.

"Yes?"

"Liza!" the voice on the other end boomed out. "This is Bob Clawson!"

She had not seen him since the Rotarian picnic four years ago, but Liza remembered the high-school principal well: the ample belly, the prissy three-piece suit he had worn, coat and all, all through that hot July day, fearful of betraying his dignity to the handful of high-school students who had shown up with their parents. "Good to hear your voice," Liza said courteously. "Can I help you?"

"Actually, it was Creath I wanted to speak to."

"Creath is putting in an extra hour at the ice plant."

"Bull for work? Eh? Well, that's good. That's fine. I can call again another time."

"May I tell him what this is about?" Liza was curious now, because Bob Clawson was town council, Bob Clawson was white collar, Bob Clawson didn't phone up just anybody . . . and at that long-since picnic he had avoided the Buracks the way he might have avoided a rabid dog.

"Just a little group some of us are getting together," Clawson said amiably. "I heard about your speech at the Women last week. Meat and potatoes Americanism, my wife tells me. Not enough of that going around these days."

"Bad times," Liza said automatically.

"Some of us are more than a little concerned." Liza imagined who "some of us" might be: Bob Clawson knew every judge and lawyer and realtor in the county. "We wanted to get together, talk about doing something to protect the town. Thought Creath might be interested."

She felt a small thrill run through her. Of course, their rehabilitation could not be complete so soon; Clawson must have some secondary reason for wanting Creath, some dirty work he wanted done. But it was a stepping stone. She thought, we are at least on probation.

"I'm sure Creath will be anxious to talk to you," she said.

"Well, I appreciate that, Liza."

"Yes."

"Good talking to you. I'll call back, then."

"Yes." She thought of asking for his number but decided against it: better not to appear too anxious. "Thank you," she said.

She hung up the phone and leaned a moment on the dust mop, waiting for her heart to calm its aggravated beat.

Everything was happening so quickly!

The evening was naturally anxious. Creath absorbed the news without visible reaction—only smoked his cigars and played the big Atwater-Kent radio. But

Liza could tell by the way he held the paper creased in thirds, not turning the pages, that it was on his mind.

The phone rang at half past eight. Creath waited for Liza to pick it up. Bob Clawson. She passed the receiver to her husband; he motioned her out of the parlor and pushed shut the door with his foot.

Liza lingered in the hallway. She was not eavesdropping. Her posture was erect, disdainful. Still, she thought, words have a way of slipping through doors.

Tonight, however, Creath's tone was suppressed; the conversation went on a maddeningly long time, but all Liza heard was "yes" and "no" and . . . if she had made it out correctly . . . one other word.

By nine Creath was out of the parlor. He went directly to the kitchen and poured a drink of water from the tap. From the way the veins stood out on his face Liza guessed he would have preferred hard liquor. "What is it," she said, "what?"

"Nothing much," Creath said: but it was the same falsely casual tone in which he had customarily lied to her about Anna Blaise (a memory she quickly suppressed). "Just Bob Clawson getting together some bullshit—pardon me—some two-bit smoker. Bunch of men griping about the Red Menace. Harmless, I guess." He took a big swallow of water. "Guess I'll go."

Liza nodded dutifully. Secretly, however, she retained her suspicions. She did not think "two bit" would describe any organization Bob Clawson would ever bother to get involved with.

And as for "smoker"—well, that was possible. Anything was possible. But the word that had drifted through the parlor door had not sounded much like "smoker" or "two bit."

The word Liza had heard was "vigilante."

Later that evening Liza got a phone call of her own: Helena Baxter calling to let her know that the votes from the last meeting had been counted; that the results were not official, of course, until the announcement the following weekend, but—speaking strictly off the record—it looked like Liza had won a landslide victory.

Travis watched the switchman's hut from the reedy bank of the Fresnel River, dusk gathering around him like the cupped palms of two huge black hands. He hadn't eaten for two days—his money had run out and there had been nothing to scrounge at the hobo jungle—and voices circled like birds inside him.

He was not sure how he had come to this. He was dead broke, his clothes were torn and stiff with dirt, the only way he had of washing himself was to dip his body in the frigid river water. All this was foreign to him. Mama had always been scrupulously clean; she had kept their small house soaped and dusted and aired. The thought created in him a wave of nostalgia so physical it left him weak-kneed. And his traitorous memory chose that moment to echo back something Creath had said (it seemed like) a long time ago: *Well, we all know where that path inclines, I guess.*

Nancy and Anna had brought him to this, he thought. Broke, hungry, cold . . . and without the simple willpower necessary to hop a freight and put some miles in back of him. He knew what was happening in the town, he had not needed Nancy to tell him that; he had been down The Spur twice, spending the last of his pocket money on food, and on both occasions he had been paced out by the police. The jungle was overdue for a rousting—possibly, given the mood in Haute Montagne, a violent one. He *should* leave. There was nothing for him here.

But he gazed at the shack where Nancy was. Nancy and the Anna-thing.

Suppose, he thought, we *do* help her (posing the question aloud, though there was no one to hear him here in the tall grass)—suppose we *do* help her, well, what then? Where does that leave us?

Alone, he thought bitterly, broke, nowhere to go. No better off. Haute Montagne would never welcome back Travis or Nancy. Too many rules had been broken, too many borders transgressed. He shivered in his inadequate clothing and wondered if Nancy knew the kind of future she had devised for herself.

Maybe that was what was keeping him here, this remnant of what he had felt for her, this fear . . . but was it strong enough to draw him back inside that shack?

He thought of Anna: her moth-wing skin. Her eyes coldly blue in the darkness.

His love. His fear.

He might have turned away then, might have been driven back by the terrible intensity of the vision, when he saw, far off, a figure advancing from the stand of elder trees down by the switching yards. The gait was familiar but the memory eluded him: Who could be coming here? Then the name fell into place—*Greg Morrow*—and with the name a tremor of fear.

Travis emitted a sort of moan and stood up, running forward without thinking about it. He intercepted Greg halfway to the switchman's shack.

Greg looked at him warily but with an obvious contempt. Confronting him, Travis felt suddenly helpless, foolish: what could he say? "You don't have any business here," he managed.

It was inadequate, but Greg Morrow must not be allowed near the switchman's shack. Obviously he had suspicions: that was bad enough; but if he knew the truth—

But Greg was smiling. "That where she is?" — nodding toward the shack. "That whore Anna Blaise? Nancy, too, maybe?" The smile became a smirk. "You fuckin' 'em both, farmboy, is that it? You know, you smell like shit. You look like shit, you smell like shit. But, hey, maybe they like that, huh? I bet it drives 'em nuts—that stink—"

Travis balled his fists. But before he could move Greg had put his hand into his coat pocket and pulled out a knife. It was a stupid knife, Travis thought, wood-handled, with a long serrated blade; it looked like a cheap steak knife. But he guessed it could cut. Greg waved it gleefully at him, and Travis felt a wave of fear wash over him. Fear and—something else.

"Not this time," Greg said calmly. "I won't be screwed over this time. Stand still! I'm just gonna go over and knock on the door. No problem. Just want to see who's home."

He stepped forward, and Travis—hardly aware of himself—stepped in front of him. Greg stood still. The knife was motionless in his hand. Travis looked at the knife and then at Greg. Greg's eyes twinkled, there was a hint of glee there, and his smile was the rictus of a man strapped into a roller coaster, coming to the top of the first big hump and enjoying it somehow, somehow thriving on it. Travis realized then that Greg *would* use the knife, would use it gladly; that if Travis were hurt, if he died, it wouldn't matter; Travis was a hobo now, found dead, he would be quietly buried.

"Do it," he said aloud, and a part of him wondered where the words came from. His voice was guttural, very nearly a growl. "Do it, Greg. I'll take the knife away from you. I vow I will. And I'll cut your balls off with it."

Travis waited. The knife was only inches from his belly. But he looked at Greg and saw that some of the giddy hysteria had faded from his eyes. The knife wavered; an uncertainty had crept into the equation.

Then, swiftly, Greg smiled again.

He let the knife drop. "Well, I guess I know what's in there already. I guess you just told me." He took a step backward. "Have fun while you can, farmboy."

Travis watched him walk almost lazily back toward the trees, listened for the sound of the car cranking up. His own heart was beating wildly; he felt dizzy.

He thought of Nancy in the shack, of what she had so narrowly avoided. Of what she could not much longer avoid, now that Greg Morrow had come back here. Christ God, he thought, shivering, she's consorting with demons—they'll crucify her—

He turned back and there was the sound of her scream.

He pulled her away from Anna, and instantly Nancy stopped trembling. She looked up at Travis with a mute, enormous gratitude. "You *came*...."

"Nance, what is it? What's wrong?"

The gun, she thought. The fear, the agony ... She touched her ribs, her belly, wanting the reassurance that those wounds she had felt were not really her wounds. "I can't explain," she said faintly. "I don't understand it myself—"

But Anna had stopped shaking, and she sat up now, hollow-eyed, luminous with faint blue fire. Nancy felt Travis recoil; but she gripped his hand and held it tightly, needing him.

Anna blinked. Her grief had filled the room; it was palpable, physically present, a smell like roses ... a cloud ... an electricity in the skin. ...

She looked at Nancy. "You felt it?"

"Yes! God, yes!" She pressed against Travis. "That was him, wasn't it? That was Bone. He's close—"

Anna said faintly, "They're killing him."

Interlude:
Bone Loses Faith

In a little railtown called Buckton their luck went bad.

The wad of money in the right-hand pocket of Bone's navy pea coat had grown much larger. Twice in the course of this hot summer, in towns whose names they did not know, they had committed successful robberies. "Nothing big," Deacon said. "Nothing ambitious. Just a little money out of the till. Just a kind of income tax. A little Relief Program for Archie and Deacon and Bone." They would locate a gas station or a general store not too far from the railway or too close to town, would approach it at dusk; Deacon, brandishing a handgun he had taken from the Darcy farmhouse, would empty the till. The proprietor or the store clerk might weep, might curse, might silently watch; but it was never Deacon or Archie he looked at, it was Bone; Bone huge and blankly pale, his pallid wrists projecting from the cuffs of his pea coat, his eyes white and unblinking in their cavernous orbits.

This should have been the same. They had hiked away from a hobo jungle to this place, a white-washed building with a torn screen door and the word Sundries written above it. They stood outside in the gathering dusk, calculating the isolation of the place, the chance that somebody might come by. "It's wide open here," Archie said nervously. "Anybody could see us." But Deacon only favored him with a contemptuous sneer. "Cowardly talk," he said, and reached under his coat for the big handgun. "For Christ's sake," Archie began—but Deacon had already pushed through the rust-hinged door.

Bone hurried after.

The room inside was narrow, plank-floored, tidy. Sacks of flour squatted on pineboard shelves. Bone was engulfed in the heady smell of wood polish and grain, in the merciless yellow light of an overhead bulb. The proprietor was a barrel-shaped man who had not yet noticed Deacon's gun; his eyes were fixed on Bone. Bone sensed the man's distrust, not yet coalesced into fear. The proprietor said, frogthroated, "Can I help you gents?"—then paled as Deacon stepped forward, grinning.

Archie watched the door. That was his job, and he performed it flawlessly. Bone stood beside Deacon at the counter, claustrophobic in this enclosed place; Deacon held the pistol. "All we want is what's in the till," Deacon said coolly. "Hand it over slow."

"Car coming," Archie said from the door.

Deacon did not turn. "Let me know if it stops." He was relaxed, methodical. Deacon was not afraid of the man behind the counter, not afraid of jail or of committing violence. He had changed, Bone thought, since the Darcy house. Maybe he didn't *want* to kill the storekeeper, but he would not hesitate to do so should the occasion arise; some part of him might even welcome the violence, the brief wild pleasure of pulling the trigger and proclaiming his potency. Bone perceived all this without words. The immanence of death boiled around Deacon like a thundercloud. He stank of it.

The storekeeper had frozen. He stared at Deacon, at Bone, at Deacon again. Beads of sweat started out on his broad forehead.

"The till," Deacon said. "Empty the goddamn till!"

"Car gone by," Archie said.

Bone watched the storekeeper's fat hands delve into the cash drawer. He wadded the cash as he tugged it out, pushed the soiled green bills across the counter. "It's not much," he said, his voice cracking, "but it's all—see—look—"

"All right, all right." Deacon used his pistol to sweep the cash toward Bone. Bone took it without counting it and stuffed it into the pea coat.

"Archie?"

"All clear . . . no, wait, Christ, there's another car!"

Deacon held the pistol steady. On the wall, a Pepsi-Cola clock ticked out seconds. The breathing of the storekeeper was stertorous and aggrieved.

"Gone by?" Deacon asked tightly.

"It's—" Archie's voice lost a beat. "Deacon, it's slowing down."

"Be damned," Deacon said. He turned fractionally.

Bone watched as the storekeeper dived behind the counter. When he came up an instant later he had a shotgun in his hands. Deacon turned back but his comprehension lagged. Bone felt the seismic shift—Deacon's confusion and fear, the storekeeper's blossoming triumph.

The shotgun was inches from Deacon's chest. The storekeeper tightened his finger on the thick steel trigger.

Bone reached out and took the gun in one huge hand. He jerked the barrel upward. The storekeeper's finger closed convulsively and both barrels discharged into the ceiling.

"Oh my Lord," the storekeeper said. Bone snatched the weapon away from him and threw it into a corner with the stitched cotton sacks of animal feed. "Oh, my sweet Lord." And Deacon thrust forward his pistol.

"Deacon," Bone said gently. "Deacon, don't."

But it was too late. Feverish with hatred, Deacon fired.

The storekeeper lurched back gap-chested and bloody into a wall of patent medicines. Brown bottles of iron tonic fell about him like hail.

He was dead. It was that simple.

Death again, Bone thought sadly.

"Fucker tried to kill me," Deacon said, trembling. "You saw him! Can't deny it! Tried to *kill* me!"

And Bone looked at Deacon, a small man now, frightened in the aftermath of his own violence, and thought: *I don't owe him anything.*

It was a new idea, startling and absolute.

Deacon was alive now because of Bone. Bone had discharged his debt.

White smoke coiled from the barrel of Deacon's pistol.

"Tried to kill me! You saw him!"

"Car gone by," Archie said weakly.

They rode mostly empty boxcars. If they entered a crowded one, it would be empty at the next whistlestop. Bone's reputation had grown among the hoboes.

"Fuck 'em all," Deacon said cheerfully. They sat in a boxcar—empty—with the prairie night rushing past outside. It was no longer summer. The wind was cutting and Bone clutched his jacket around him. The Calling was elusive tonight.

Deacon had acquired a bottle of muscatel. He drank unstintingly and offered none to Archie. After a time, pacified, he talked in fragments about his life in Chicago, about the Great War, about the child he had abandoned. Then, with a violent finality, he passed out.

Bone and Archie sat in the rattling darkness, very nearly invisible. The door was open a crack and

Bone watched the landscape pour by. A harvest moon hung on the horizon.

"He'll do it again," Archie said.

Talking to himself, maybe, Bone thought.

"I should walk away," Archie said. "Walk away and be shut of the whole thing. I *should*. . . ."

Bone gazed at him inquisitively.

"Ah, no," Archie said, taking up the remainder of Deacon's muscatel. "No. I guess I've been with him too long. Maybe you don't understand that. It's not queer. Don't get that idea. It's just that I owe him some things."

Bone nodded.

"I was never good on my own. Too damn dumb. Deacon's a thinker. Smart. Smart as a whip! But that's where he gets into trouble. Figuring angles all the time can make a person crazy. I'm not trying to stir up trouble, but listen, Bone, listen to me: to Deacon you're just one more angle . . . you know what I mean?"

There was no fear about Archie now, only a sadness, a melancholy, like the scent of the rain in the air. Bone said, "I know."

"It's been sweet for him so far. Christ, he could do anything! He was right. He *was* right. It's not Deacon they see, it's Bone, the geek—you. Deacon's sitting pretty." The chill air made him shiver, and Archie took up the bottle and swallowed convulsively. "You, though, Bone, you're out in the cold, you know that? Out in the snow and ice. When they hang somebody, it won't be Deacon. And pretty soon Deacon's gonna want to lose you. Oh, yes. They know you now. Hoboes know you, cops know you. Everybody. You're getting to be a liability. Bad to be with. You're not much good to him anymore."

It was true enough, Bone thought. But he guessed it didn't really matter any longer. He had paid out his debt to Deacon. It worked both ways: Deacon was bad for Bone to be with, as well.

But he worried about being alone, about being recognized . . . especially now that he was so close.

The Calling was faint but very near. In recent days his mind had seemed to race; he was filled with a new lucidity. He understood so much.

"I'll stick with him," Archie was saying. "I don't care what he did. I know he killed those people. By God, didn't we bury them? But he needs me." Archie looked at Bone pleadingly. "He needs me . . . doesn't he? Doesn't he?"

"I guess he does," Bone said.

They spent the next night outside a freightyard, camped by themselves, huddled over a weak fire while the wind came sluicing over the prairie. "Give me the money," Deacon said, drunk again.

Bone, shivering, pulled the wad of bills out of his pocket.

Deacon counted it twice. It came to almost three hundred dollars.

Deacon gripped the fluttering bills tightly, as if the wind might carry them off. "We could go a long way on this," he said. "A *long* way. Some warm place. Florida, maybe. What say, Archie? We spend the winter in Florida. Live like goddamn kings. Buy a piece of property maybe."

"There's no Florida property for three hundred bucks," Archie said morosely.

"Then we'll get more," Deacon said.

Archie looked at Bone and then back at Deacon. "If you mean—hey, Deacon, I don't think we should—"

"One more time," Deacon said. "Maybe someplace a little ritzier. Someplace they keep more cash in the till. Someplace—"

"No!" Astonishingly, Archie had risen to his feet. "Deacon, it's crazy! They'll spot him a mile away! We'll all be killed, all of us!"

Deacon didn't answer, only sat back against his rucksack and gazed at Archie. In a moment Archie's rage had faded; he looked foolish, outlined against the stars with the night wind picking at his tattered coat, and he sat back down again.

"Just one more," Deacon said. His voice was placid, calming. "I know we can't carry on with it. All I want is a little extra. You understand. A little something to keep us warm. Something to keep the cold away. You understand, Archie."

But Archie was shivering, Archie was hugging himself, and it looked to Bone as if Archie might not be warm ever again.

He woke up that night after the fire had gone out.

The embers were cold, the ground beneath him was cold. Bone sat up and hugged his pea coat around himself.

Amber light from the freightyard washed out over the prairie. Behind a chain link fence, an acetylene torch dropped showers of sparks. The night air was full of metallic smells and the stars above him were icy and strange.

The Calling sang to him.

Here I am, find me.
Now before the time passes.
Bone, find me, here, now.

He could not mistake the urgency of it. He sensed that some irreversible process had been set in motion, that he needed to play out his part. His body felt huge and strange about him. In this last week the sickness had come back, the convulsions that bowed him heel-to-crown as if he were about to erupt from this clumsy cocoon and burst forth transfigured. It was time to move on. *So close now*. He did not need words to know it.

He moved away from the cold campfire, from the prone bodies of Archie and Deacon, into the darkness. In the shadow of a rust-eaten oil canister he stood to his full height and scanned the eastern horizon.

She was a light there.

He thought it for the first time: "She."

She was a blue corona that rose and flared like a searchlight against the stars. Bone knew without thinking it that the light would be invisible to Archie or Deacon. It was a sign meant exclusively for Bone, a kind of marker. *Here I am*. He trembled with the closeness of it.

The light transfixed him, consumed all his attention for a timeless moment, and he was startled when Archie tapped his shoulder.

The smaller man was shaking. His knapsack was in his hand. He gazed up at Bone, and there were tears leaking from his eyes.

"We leave him here," Archie whispered. "Listen to me. Without us he can't hurt himself. He'll be okay. We leave him here, right, Bone? Without us they can't touch him. He'll be okay—"

And Bone, gazing at Archie, was overcome with another realization.

He was not like Archie or Deacon. *I am not human*. The thought was dizzying, and for a moment he was afraid a convulsion might overtake him. In the glare of that blue light he had glimpsed himself, had bathed for a moment in the secret illumination of the Jeweled World. Bone's comprehension failed him, but he understood, at least, that he was not like Archie. The gulf between them was vast, vast. . . .

"Archie, no," he said. His voice seemed loud in the darkness. "I have to go—"he pointed helplessly—"*there*—"

Archie gazed beyond him, not listening, blind to the Calling light. "He changed since we met you. But that's not true, either. It was nothing you did. Just something he saw in you. I don't know. You were like the ghost of all the beatings he took. But not beaten. All his old anger came out."

There was a motion in the darkness beyond the oil tanks. Bone, distracted, looked away.

"I guess I changed too," Archie said. "I only ever wanted to help him. I guess you know what I mean. But I can't do that by staying with him. That's the hard part." His eyes focused on Bone. There was angish there but also a kind of strength. Bone felt a shadow of the smaller man's pain, of this hard-won pcacc he had arrived at, somehow, in the deep of the night. "We have to leave him. It's the only way to help him. Christ, it frightens me to be alone! It's the only thing I was ever really scared of. But if we don't leave him, Bone, he'll kill himself. He's drugged up on crazy vengeance and there's no sense in him."

That motion again—a flicker of denim, a sigh like drawn breath. Bone's hackles rose. He turned to the smaller man beside him. "Archie—"

But there was an explosion that lit up the night. Bone was momentarily blinded, and when his vision cleared he saw Archie on his knees, gagging, and then Archie in a pool of his own dark blood, limply dead.

Deacon stepped out from behind the oil tanks with the pistol in his hand.

He turned on his heel, and the pistol was aimed now at Bone.

The immensity of the betrayal shocked him. Deacon had shot Archie. Archie, who had held his mirror when he shaved. Archie, who had loved him.

"He's dead," Bone stammered out.

Deacon nodded. His eyes were wide, his pupils dilated. "Sure he's dead. I caught him. Son of a bitch! Run away on me, would he? Run away on Deacon?"

"He was afraid for you." Bone shook his head, aghast. "He was afraid you might get caught."

"Don't move!" Deacon thrust the pistol forward. "I heard you two talking! Move out, he said,

leave Deacon behind, he said, that's what you were
doing out here in the night—"

"The pistol shot," Bone managed. "The men in
the railyard. They'll be here soon."

On the horizon, the blue Calling light guttered
and flared.

"He was just waiting for his chance," Deacon
said. "Sneak off and leave Deacon in the lurch. Son
of a bitch! I guess I know better."

"He loved you."

"That's a dirty lie." Deacon pressed the gun forward. There were voices now from the railyard, and
his expression hardened. "Give me the money."

But Deacon had the smell of death about him, a
carrion stench Bone could not ignore. He had seen
the Jeweled World, the bright beauty of it, and he
could only recoil in horror from the ugly thing Deacon had become.

Deacon, he understood, meant to kill him.

"*Now*," Deacon said.

Bone darted his big hand toward the pistol. He
could not grasp it but only slapped it away. The gun
flew through the cold air while Deacon cursed and
leaped after it. "I'll kill you," Deacon panted, "I'll
kill you, you geek bastard!"

Bone stumbled backward. The sheer scope of it
defied understanding. Deacon had killed Archie—
here was the steaming carcass to prove it—and now
Deacon meant to kill Bone.

There was no one, Bone thought bitterly. No one
and nothing he could trust here. Only the Calling.
Only the light and the song of it. Nothing human.
He was not human, and there was nothing in the
human world for him.

Only danger here.

Deacon scrabbled for the gun, and Bone turned
and ran.

The scissorbills ambushed him at the hobo jungle.

The came at him with flashlights and guns. He was trapped, encircled suddenly, blinded. His foot caught in a railway tie and he fell clumsily among the gravel and embers. There were four flashlights, bright bobbing flares that disguised the faces behind them, but more men than that, maybe more guns. He stood up slowly and listened to the awe that crept into their voices as they made a ring around him.

"Big bastard, ain't he?"

"It's him, all right—"

"No question."

" —the one they wrote about in the papers—"

"Christ, *look* at him!"

They pushed him up against the corrugated side of a reefer car.

"He's not packing anything." A man stepped forward, and Bone saw his face in the reflected light. Thick, grizzled face. Save for the uniform this might have been one of the hoboes. Bone felt that same gulf again, a revulsion, a blossoming hatred. Such men had beaten him too often before. But now now, not now: he was too close.

The scissorbill shone a light in Bone's eyes, and the others pressed close behind him. The heat and smell of them were unbearable. "We heard a pistol fired," the man said. "Same pistol killed all those farmfolks maybe? Huh? You want to tell us where it is?"

There were no words to answer. Bone shook his head.

The scissorbill grinned and brought his knee up between Bone's legs.

Bone doubled over with the pain of it.

"Think," the man said. "Oh, we'll hand you over to the cops soon enough. They'll lock you up somewhere—a long, long time—assuming they don't choose to hang you. But we got you first. And nobody cares if we have a little fun of our own."

The Calling was suddenly strong in him, stronger than it had ever been before, not a song now but a river of need, a torrent. Bone felt a convulsion coming on. He was full of that wild energy. But he did not convulse.

What happened next happened quickly. He straightened, and the pain and the betrayal and the hatred in him rose to a terrifying crest. He screamed, a high-pitched falsetto scream. And he swung out his fist.

It should have been a futile gesture. It was not. The actinic blue Calling light shone now from inside him. It was electric, an aura, and he knew from their eyes that these men *could* see it. Bone swung his arm, touching them, full of violent energy, and where he touched them the blue light leaped from the apex of his arm, and the men he touched were gone, then—dead, he supposed, but more than that, quite literally vanished, dispatched (he could not say how he knew this) to the nothingness that lay between the worlds.

His sense of time deserted him. He supposed it only took a moment. When he finished there was no one left around him. In the darkness, he heard Deacon calling his name.

"Bone!"

He ran for a moving freight. He was weary, confused, intoxicated with the Calling. Cattle cars slid by him, gathering speed, shuttering bars of light into the morning mist. Bone tripped and fell forward, stumbled up again. All these cars were closed and locked.

"Bone! Give it back, you bastard!"

The money, Bone thought. It was still in his jacket pocket. Was that all Deacon wanted—the money? If he had it, would he let Bone leave?

Bone hesitated and turned back. Deacon was a shadow running alongside this redball freight. The gun was still in his hand. "Deacon—" Bone said.

And Deacon fired the pistol.

The bullet took Bone in the upper thigh. He roared, twisted, fell. The pain was immense. It spread through him like wildfire, and he could not dismiss it. Rage rose up like sour bile inside him. A second bullet struck sparks from the pebbles near his head, and Bone reached up wildly.

His huge hand caught in the undercarriage of the accelerating freight. It was as if an undertow had taken him. He was dragged forward, Deacon shouting incoherently, and the railway ties gouged cruelly at him. He lifted himself desperately, hooked a foot up.

Deacon fired again, and the bullet scored a bloody pathway up Bone's prominent rib cage. Two of the ribs were broken instantly. White fire clutched at his heart.

He pulled himself up, screaming. This was a reefer car. No good to him—unless the ice compartment was empty. He inched backward, clinging with his long arms like an insect. His good blue pea coat was wet with blood.

"Bone, goddamn you—" But Deacon's voice was fading now. The train picked up speed.

Groaning, Bone let himself into the ice compartment. His breathing was labored, and he felt on the verge of a great darkness. In one last lunging effort he secured the lid so it would not lock and fell back on the hard wire-mesh. He lost consciousness at once.

Bone dreamed.

In his dreams the Calling light glimmered and flashed, illuminating a horizon he could not see. There was a face he did not recognize—a woman's face. Her mouth moved, framing a word. *Bone.* So close now.

He saw Deacon's face, too, transformed and vulpine, jaws agape, slavering; and Bone was suffused with a contempt and a hatred so immense that his thinking mind closed against it. Pain and hatred merged, a single great conflagration, lightless but full of heat.

The train bent into a curve. Bone's huge body shifted; agony flared. The cold had numbed him, but his wounds were deep. He turned on his side, breathing shallowly. His dreams were full of death.

The train slowed—an endless time later—and the Calling woke him.

He fell from the reefer car into blindness and pain.

The train sighed and groaned, slowing. It was dark here. He could not say how much time had passed. He blinked, motionless, the agony in his leg and chest beating at him. Dark here, by all human perception—but the Calling light was lustrous in the sky *(so close)* and cast an eerie illumination over the tall dry grass, the distant railway trestle.

Bone crept into a shallow depression where the prairie grass hid him.

Close now, Bone thought. So close. So close. He held his left hand closed across his chest wound. The blood in his blue Navy pea coat (torn now, ruined) had begun to crystallize. Weakness flooded him.

I'll go, he thought. Not far. He stood erect. The stars watched him. The wind bit and probed.

Bone took a halting step forward, another . . . but the pain welled up again, irresistible now; and Bone toppled forward into the wild grass; the prairie swallowed him up; Bone closed his eyes, and the stars went dark.

Chapter Fourteen

They kept a vigil through the night.

Anna was often unconscious. The blue light played fitfully over her. At times she seemed awake but oblivious to them, her lips moving wordlessly, her eyes dilated. Travis closed his eyes briefly, and it seemed to him that the room was in some way still visible, but filled with strange translucent shapes, pale emeralds, impossibly faceted diamonds. He sat erect and closed his hand on Nancy's; they did not speak.

By morning the crisis had passed. A wan daylight filtered through the wallboards. Anna lay in a heap on her mattress—diminished, Travis thought, rice-paper white, stick-thin, only her eyes animate. She sat up, blinking.

Nancy cleared her throat.

"Anna? Is he—is Bone dead?"

"No," the alien woman said. "Not quite."

"He's hurt?"

"Yes."

"Still coming?"

"Still coming. Very close now."

"Is there anything we can do?"

"Not for a time."

Nancy stood up wearily. There were dark bruises of sleeplessness under her eyes. She stretched. "I'm going to the river to wash. Travis? You'll be okay here?"

He nodded slowly.

Sunlight washed inward as Nancy opened the door. She left it ajar, and Travis watched her descend the slope of the riverbank. In a moment she was out of sight.

He looked back at Anna Blaise.

Now, he thought. If he ever hoped to sort this out, now was the time. While she was weak . . . too weak, perhaps, to lie.

"It's all true, then? What you told Nancy, I mean, about another world and—all that?"

"Can you look at me and doubt it?"

She was no longer beautiful, Travis thought, but her voice retained its grace, its seductiveness. Maybe its deceit. "Nancy is sometimes credulous."

"You were the one who told her I wasn't human."

"There is no question of that," Travis said. "But there are other questions. Nancy believes you mean no harm. Maybe. But this Bone. There have been stories in the papers—"

"Bone is credulous, too. But not evil."

"We only have your word for that."

"I'm sorry. What else can I offer?"

She was motionless, not even blinking. Travis guessed she was conserving her strength. He said, "You didn't mean to come here?"

"Not in this fashion. It was a mistake."

"Nancy said you and, uh, Bone got separated—"

"The journey between worlds is arduous even for us. There are storms in the chaos between. A misstep in that labyrinth can be a disaster. Yes, we were separated."

"How come—if that's true—how come nobody came after you?"

She smiled faintly. "There are more worlds than mine and yours. We were lucky to arrive within the boundaries of a single continent. Bone searched. The time passed. That's all. Together we can travel back."

"Even if he's hurt?"

She frowned, shrugged.

"I don't understand," Travis said. "If it's so hard, so dangerous—why do any of this? Why come here?"

"Why would anyone travel between worlds? To learn. Do you understand that, Travis? To acquire . . ."

"—knowledge?"

"*Wisdom.*"

The sound of Nancy's singing traveled up from the riverbank. The sun had warmed the air a little. Travis looked almost fearfully into Anna's huge eyes, but there was nothing there to betray her. Nothing that said *this is the truth* or *this is a lie.* "Anna Blaise doesn't exist, then."

"I am Anna Blaise."

"But it's false. A mask."

She folded her hands in her lap. Her legs were crossed; she looked, Travis thought, like a frail Buddha. "I am not human. But I have a certain access to human minds. Anna Blaise is in some sense a metaphor of myself, the way a name might be translated into a foreign language. But, Travis, see: if I give back a human appearance it can only be a sort of reflection. A mirror, not a mask."

Travis had begun to sweat, he was not sure why. The air was still cold. "You weren't a mirror for Creath Burack."

"But I was! I had to be! How else to survive, to claim his protection?"

"A mirror—"

"Of his deepest needs. Unspoken. Unadmitted. Creath Burack is a deep well of desires and fears—all buried, hidden."

Travis said hoarsely, "You used him." He was suddenly frightened again. The lines of her face were fluid, mobile; he was afraid of what he might see there.

She said defiantly, "I traded my body for his protection when I was helpless. Which of us used the other, Travis?"

Her voice had subtly changed; it was hauntingly familiar. He said, "That's dirty—that's—"

"An old, old bargain. I'm not the first to have made it. And I will not be blamed for it."

Travis stood up.

He recognized the face now. The face and the voice. "Who's talking?" he demanded, his own voice shrill and childish. "Who's saying this? You—or my mother?"

"Both of us, I imagine," Anna said.

Nancy returned, her hair wet, and pushed through the flimsy wooden door. She saw Travis sitting bolt upright, staring. Anna was as inscrutable as ever.

"Travis?" she said. "Something wrong?"

"No," he said. "No," and went to the door. "I'll be back." Taking his own turn, she guessed, at the riverside.

Nancy settled down in the shadows, exhausted. "What happened?"

Anna pivoted her head to face her. "Travis wanted to know some things."

"He gave you the third degree?" She was quietly shocked—surely Anna was too frail for that sort of treatment.

But the alien woman said, "He needed reassurance. I cannot say whether he received it."

"You told him about being a mirror?"

"Yes. Though I think he understood it, intuitively, long before this."

Nancy closed her eyes. She needed sleep more than anything. Too much had happened. Weariness moved like a tide in her. "You're that woman," she heard herself saying, "the one you say he dreams about—"

"The pale woman. Travis sees her in me, yes. I give back that part of him—that fear, that desire."

Nancy stifled a yawn. "And what about me? What do I see in you?"

Anna gazed back . . . frail, emaciated, cast out; like a piece of flotsam, Nancy thought sleepily, washed up on some uncaring reef. . . .

"Only yourself," Anna said gently.

When she woke it was past nightfall again. Nancy had slept sitting up; her back was stiff and she was cold. She had to get back to town, she thought. Her mother might have called the police. Anything might have happened.

Travis was beside her.

"We can't stay here," he said. "Greg Morrow saw me last night. If he wants to make trouble there's not much we can do about it."

"Where else is there to go? Anyway—" She stretched. "—we can't move Anna. It would kill her. There's not much left of her but her bones."

Bones and that terrible light. Anna sat cross-legged on the mattress, hardly breathing. Her eyes were rolled back into her head.

Nancy felt a twinge of concern. "Anna—?"

"He's near here," Anna Blaise said suddenly. "He's very near here indeed."

And she blinked and looked intently at Travis.

Chapter Fifteen

Creath Burack was careful to park his battered Ford pickup two blocks beyond Bob Clawson's modest house on DeVille Street. He did not want to be conspicuously odd-man-out among all the fine automobiles parked there. There would be enough of that to come, he thought.

He did not relish this meeting.

His gut burned, though he had eaten sparingly at dinner. He sat for a breathless moment gripping the steering wheel as the Ford's engine cooled.

There are limits, he thought. There are limits beyond which I will not go. He wasn't stupid; he knew the kind of fear that was sweeping the town. It was impossible to miss. The times had gone sour. There were unemployed men everywhere, families starving, farms turned to dust, murders and gangsterism and reckless talk of revolution. And men like Bob Clawson and his cronies—men of money or, failing that, of staunch propriety—were the scaredest of all.

He thought: I do not know what they want from me. But there are limits.

He climbed out of the automobile.

Liza had made him wear his best Sunday suit. Creath regretted that decision now. The collar

nagged at him; the old-fashioned vest was conspicuously tight across his belly. It wore on him like an
admission of inadequacy. He gritted his teeth and
paced out the necessary steps to the Clawson house.

Clawson's wife, a gushy, nervous woman ad-
dicted to the wearing of gloves, met him at the door.
"Why, Creath," she said, "so good to see you," and
led him to the parlor. "The men are all inside. Go
on!"

There were times, Creath wanted to say, when
you would have crossed the street to avoid me. But
he only mumbled, "Yes, Evie, thanks," and held his
hat in his hand.

"The men," as she had called them, were clus-
tered around a dining room table. The shades had
been pulled and the electric lights switched on. The
air was already blue with cigar smoke. Creath entered, and the rumble of male voices tapered to a
stillness.

He felt the sweat tickling down his ribs.

Bob Clawson pushed forward. The high-school
principal looked dowdy and small among these lawyers and realtors and store owners. There was a
primness in him he could not shake. But his hail-
fellow smile and his extended right hand made
Creath feel stupidly grateful. He took Clawson's
hand eagerly. It moved, wetly alive in his grip, like
some kind of hairless animal.

"Creath Burack! Good you could make it! You
know most of these people, I think?"

By reputation mainly, Creath thought, but
Clawson's welcome had taken him out of the spot-
light, and he was pleased to see the faces turn incuriously away from him, the rumble of
conversation resume. He would have liked to be invisible.

"Sure," he said breathlessly.

"I really am pleased you could make it. We've
been having a lot of discussions here you might find
interesting. I think it's important that people like

ourselves get together in a time like this, don't you?"

"I guess so," Creath said.

"But surely you've noticed it, too? But then it's all the more obvious from where I sit. I see the young people. Your wife made some astute points in that regard, I understand, in her little speech. I assume you agree with her."

Creath had not heard the speech. Liza had told him about it. He had listened with only half an ear. It had sounded like the same old stuff to him. The country was going to hell in a handbasket, true enough—but he could not arouse himself to be shocked by it.

"I go along with her a hundred percent," he said, and wondered miserably if he ought to have come at all. He did not like these men and he was certain they had not petitioned to have him here; he was here on sufferance strictly. Then why *had* he come? Because of Liza, he thought—her stern conviction that this would better them in some way. And for more pragmatic reasons. There in the corner with a glass of brandy was his banker, a man named Crocket, who held the mortgage on his house; seated at the table was Jeff Baines, the realtor to whom Creath must turn when, inevitably, it came time to sell the ice plant; and there by the potted Chinese evergreen was Jim St. Hubert, the undertaker who would one day escort him into the cold weedy soil up at Glen Acres. In pieces and fragments these men owned him. He was beholden to them.

Clawson seemed to sense his discomfort. He poured Creath a drink from a bottle of Canadian blend. "It's important, times like this, to mend fences. Man to man. We hang together or we will hang separately. You understand?"

In truth he did not. He murmured, "Yes."

"That's good. That's fine. You finish your drink, all right? Pretty soon I'll make my little speech."

* * *

There were chairs for everyone. Creath sat at the back, bent almost double in his effort to remain inconspicuous. The room had grown unbearably hot and his body, under these layers of dark cloth, was slick with sweat. Bob Clawson's "little speech," once begun, showed no signs of winding down.

The sentiments were all familiar. Vice and sedition were abroad in the land, and the law was helpless to deal with it. "I don't mean that as any kind of slur on the work of Tim Norbloom there. We've talked, haven't we, Tim?—and he agrees that something more has to be done. I want to emphasize that we are working in privacy here. The nature of the work demands it. Many of us are public servants, Tim Norbloom and myself are just two examples, and our work might be compromised if word of this got out. But we are willing to assume that risk. We assume it because we know what every right-thinking citizen in Haute Montagne must at least suspect: that hard times call for hard action."

Creath drained the teacup of whiskey Clawson had given him, closed his eyes to better feel the alcohol working. He found himself impatient with Clawson's fine rhetoric. You can't bullshit a bullshitter. By God, he thought, I know what you are dressing up with your fine perfume.

And he thought quite involuntarily of Greg Morrow. *I know where she is.*

Was that possible? Anna Blaise still in town, still here in Haute Montagne—could that be?

He closed his eyes. Her face was there in the inner darkness.

"We are all aware," Clawson said, "of the way unemployed men and railway transients have been gathering on the outskirts of town. This has not been a pressing problem, though many of us do worry about the safety of our women, and I think we've all been more astute about locking our doors lately. I know I have—haven't you?"

Heads nodded. Creath forced open his eyes, stared glazedly at the scuffed tips of his shoes.

"But the problem may be of greater proportion than we have suspected. I'm talking about the outright seduction of our daughters. I'm talking about young girls making clandestine visits to the shantytown at the railway trestle. I'm talking about what can only be described as a very real and terrible danger to the lives and morals of our children."

Clawson paused, and there was the embracing silence of absolute attention.

"Fortunately," he said, "one of our young people has been courageous enough to step forward with this information. The problem is not yet widespread, but it could become so. And that is why we must come together."

Creath stood up. He did not mean to. Some instinct impelled him, or the liquor. "Who do you mean? Who came to you?"

Heads turned. He thought: dear God, what have I done?

Bob Clawson looked at him uneasily. "A former student at the high school," he said quickly, "and I've taken the liberty of asking him to join us so you all can meet him and hear what he has to say." Clawson opened the parlor doors behind him. "Come on in, son."

Greg Morrow stepped inside, smiling.

The rest of it was hazy in Creath's mind, a blur of perception. Greg described the assignations he had witnessed, or claimed to have witnessed, down by the railway trestle. Clawson added something about "the obligation—no, the *duty* we feel to do something about this while we can," and then the mounting burble of voices. Creath stood in a corner, smiling falsely when he could force himself to do so, drawing strength from the reassuring confluence of the two walls.

Then, an eternity later, as these well-dressed and authoritative men of means began to filter out one by one, Bob Clawson approached him with his hand once more extended.

"Creath, I know you're as concerned about these issues as the rest of us. For your own sake and Liza's. And I want you to know you can be a big help to us."

No, Creath thought. Leave me out of it. I will not be a party to this thing. It was true, he had wanted a reckoning with Anna Blaise, had wished he could expunge her from his life altogether (because, in all truth, the wanting of her was still huge within him: Christ God, he thought, I want her even now, even now)—but there was no redemption in what these men wanted, only some filthy act of violence born out of their fear and their boredom.

I am not a saint, Creath thought. He had done many things he was not proud of. He had hurt people. He would gladly have killed Travis Fisher . . . would yet, perhaps. But not this.

He thought: she could be out there.

I know where she is.

"A big help," Bob Clawson was saying, his hand on Creath's shoulder. "A husky man like yourself. And don't think it won't be noticed. We are all friends—all of us who sat in this room and pledged ourselves to the betterment of the community. And friends do things for friends. I think you must understand that."

No, Creath thought. Debts forgiven, considerations made; it was tantalizing but insufficient. No, he thought, not even for that. I won't—

But he saw Greg Morrow gazing at him across the oaken table, that insolent smile playing faintly across his lips. And he understood then that Greg Morrow was smarter than he had thought. Greg Morrow understood the tidal flow of wealth and power in Haute Montagne, how to use and manipulate it: Greg Morrow, humble as his station was, had invaded the Byzantine social structure of the town's prime movers . . . had done this terrible thing quite consciously. Greg, catching his eye, smiled oh-so-faintly. And Creath understood. The communication was explicit. *Crawl*, the smile said. *Crawl like you made me crawl. Crawl for the rich men, or you can kiss your shitty business and your swivel chair and your cheap cigars good-bye. Because these men will break you.*

Creath tore his eyes away.

Bob Clawson frowned. "We *can* count on you, can't we, Creath? It means a lot to all of us. After that wonderful speech your wife gave, I wouldn't want to think you'd backed out on us."

Creath felt his lower lip trembling. He was afraid he might begin to cry. The textured fleur-de-lis wallpaper threatened to close in about him. He needed to be out of this place.

"Yeah," he said faintly. "You can count on me."

Greg's smile broadened, and Creath fumbled for the door.

Chapter Sixteen

That night there was frost on the brittle stalks of prairie grass. Anna was sleeping or comatose, and Travis ate a sparing meal of saltines, chipped beef, and tepid water. She woke at dawn.

The last of her humanity was draining from her. The flesh was taut over her skull, and the skull itself had taken on new contours, a kind of streamlining. Her soiled dress hung limply, and Travis did not wish to know what transformations it might conceal. Her aura pulsed about her; the irises of her eyes had expanded; she gazed at him from azure depths, unfathomable. He began, "You have to leave this place. Listen: Greg Morrow knows we're here. He's bound to make trouble. Maybe when Nancy gets back we can take you over to the railway trestle. We—"

But Anna was shaking her head. When she spoke her voice, too, was more nakedly alien, a kind of soft keening; it stood up his hackles, though all she said was, *"No."*

"You don't understand. You're in danger here."

"In danger anywhere, surely? But, Travis, the time is very near. I cannot leave this place. Listen to me. Bone is close by. But he's wounded. He needs help."

Travis sat back on his haunches. It had been the coldest night of this autumn, and his jacket was inadequate, the barnboard walls of the switchman's shack thin as paper. Anna did not shiver; Travis did. "Near here?"

"Very near."

"Then go to him."

She tilted her head. "Look at me. If I stood up, the bones would break."

He nodded slowly. It was undeniable. He ventured, "I could carry you—"

"We've touched before, Travis. And I'm less human now. Human by willpower mostly. It would be difficult for you. Besides, we'll need some shelter for the duration of the Change. The shack would be best." She added, "I can describe the place where he is. But there are other things you need to know."

Travis narrowed his eyes. The candlelight flickered. He thought, she will warn me about him. All this sounded sincere, and he believed much of what she had already told him, but her very strangeness made her impossible to evaluate; the truth, as much as lies, could be a manipulation. He said, "Tell me."

"He's been wounded. The wounds are severe. He is not dead—he need not die—but he is very nearly delirious. He has also been betrayed, and in the delirium is buried his anger. This is a dangerous combination. Approaching him cannot be anything but dangerous. Bone is very strong, even wounded. And there is more."

"What?"

"He has much the same power of reflection as myself, though he exercises it differently. Travis, you need to understand how it is for us in the place we come from. We're not two separate beings. We—"

"I know," Travis said. "Nancy told me."

"Then hear it again and try to understand. You think of us as male and female, Bone and me, because we've assumed those avatars. This is terribly misleading. We're *one* person. We're separate because when we came here we had not yet achieved physical union, though we were already paired, paired here—" she touched her head, "which is why I have been able to Call him. Apart, neither of us is whole."

"Male and female," Travis said. "I don't see how it's so different."

"But you *are* different," Anna said fervently, "all of you! You're male and female both at once! Whole from birth! There *is* no purity, no perfection. A human woman distilled of all her maleness would be inconceivable, insupportable, a kind of monster—"

"Like you," Travis said.

She nodded calmly. "Like me."

"And Bone—"

"He has assumed a masculine persona. And, Travis, he is quite capable of functioning as a mirror. You look at me and I give back your own most fundamental comprehension of a woman. Yes? But Bone may be much more difficult to confront. Not just because he's wounded. Look at him, Travis, and what he will give you back is yourself. Your own deepest, hidden face. And I cannot honestly promise that you will be strong enough to confront it."

He turned away from her. The door of the shack had fallen open, and he was able to see a long way out into the fading night, the cold plains of the stars. There was the sound of wind and water running.

He didn't want to do this—any of this. He thought of all the warm, lit places of the town. *Your own face*, she had said. *Your own deepest, hidden face.* And if he saw that, he wondered, would he understand? Would he know then what had brought him here, why he was huddling in this abandoned shack, an outcast, when he could have been warm, safe, loved?

She was veiled in the flickering darkness. Goddamn her, Travis thought. She had lured him here; he had broken on the reefs of her.

An old, old bargain . . . which of us used the other?

But there was only one way out of it now. A transformation, she had said, once begun, must be completed. He guessed that was probably true. "Describe the place," Travis said.

Solemnly, she did so. The trestle, the river, the distant silhouette of the grain elevators. "Do you know where that is, Travis?"

He pulled his flimsy jacket around himself and stood up. "I know," he said.

The morning was very cold.

The sun rode up high but ineffectual over the town of Haute Montagne.

Home, Nancy had gathered up the last of her money and a change of clothes and folded them into a linen bundle. She tucked an old tintype photograph of her father into her pastille box and clicked shut the lid. She supposed this was a kind of leave-taking, a final good-bye . . . but she must not think about that.

At the foot of the stairs her mother was waiting, standing between Nancy and the front door, her face doughy and pale where it was not touched with feverish highlights of red.

"Stay," Faye Wilcox said. "You'd be mad to go out again now."

"Mama, please," Nancy began.

"I hear things," her mother said. "I am not in the position I once was. But I hear things. Things are happening in this town. Your name is mentioned." She licked her lips and seemed for a moment to lose her way . . . as if, Nancy thought, her rope bridge of words and phrases had collapsed beneath her. "It's not for myself," she said finally, softly. "I'm worried what could happen. People are talking about guns."

"I'll be careful," Nancy said.

"You were right, you know. What you said last time. He's *not* dead. Or he wasn't when he left. He just left. Left, I guess, the way you're leaving." She looked up from the floor. "Is it so awful here?"

"Not awful at all," Nancy said, feeling five years old.

"Was it my fault?"

"No."

"Well." She straightened her shoulders. "If you go, you ought not to come back. I don't mean that to be cruel. The way the town is . . ."

"I know."

"I wish I had some money to give you."

"I'll be all right," Nancy said. "I have to go."

And Faye Wilcox stood aside, though the motion seemed to pain her.

At twenty past noon Jacob Bingham, the owner and proprietor of Bingham's Hardware Store—located conveniently on the busy 200s block of Lawson Spur—smiled at Bob Clawson, the high-school principal, who had just sailed through the big front door like an autumn breeze.

Clawson made a show of examining the electrical fans, the steel-bladed lawn mowers, the fishing reels and fly rods. Then, smiling, he presented himself at the cash counter. Dressed to the nines, as usual. In the glass display case there was a selection of Bowie knives.

"Fine knives," Clawson commented.

"Wonderful knives," Jacob said amiably. "Do anything for you. Open a tin can, gut a fish, slit your throat. In the market?"

"No," Clawson said, "I guess not now. You have that package ready for me?"

Jacob brought it forth from the storage drawer beneath the counter. The package was heavy and it was wrapped in brown paper. It smelled slightly oily. He smiled. "Watch yourself, now."

Clawson extended both arms and Jacob loaded him down.

"We're very much in your debt," Clawson said.

Jacob Bingham frowned. "I understood there would be payment?"

"Of course," Clawson said hastily. "I was speaking metaphorically."

"Well. Don't fall down with that, now. You need help with the door?"

"I'll be fine."

Jacob watched him leave. Cool air swirled in the door as Clawson struggled out.

It was shaping up to be a fine day, he thought. A fine autumn day.

Outside, in his car—half past noon by the clock on the civic building—Bob Clawson plucked at the brown binding twine until the knot unraveled, then spread back the oily leaves of paper. Thus revealed, the two .22-gauge hunting rifles lay in his lap, greased and slick, alien things. He had not personally handled a rifle before. The complexity of slots and levers was daunting. But surely it could not be as complicated as it looked. One aims, he thought. One fires.

He saw Tim Norbloom's police car in his rear-view mirror. The police car pulled abreast of him, and Clawson rolled down his window, conscious of the weight of the guns in his lap.

"Pleasant day," Norbloom said, his big Nordic horseface framed in the darkness of the patrol car.

Clawson suppressed the instinctive distaste he felt for the man. "Very nice. Indian summer."

"Everything on for tonight?"

"Oh, yes."

"Bingham came through?"

"Yes, indeed."

"Then I'll be seeing you later."

"We're gathering at eight," Clawson said.

"Yessir." Norbloom shot him a mock salute. "I'll be there."

Clawson smiled perfunctorily and paused to savor the excitement growing inside him.

Liza watched with great trepidation as Creath brought up his hunting rifle—disused these many years—from the basement, and began to clean and oil it. He bent to the task like a man possessed, his eyes intently focused, and when she spoke to him he did not respond.

Surely there was nothing dangerous in this? Liza felt as if events had somehow gone beyond her . . . but surely Bob Clawson would not be party to do an enterprise that was physically dangerous?

"Creath," she said tentatively. "Creath, if this is something . . . if you don't feel you should be involved. . . ."

But he lifted his head to gaze at her, and the expression on his face was a combination of implacability and silent horror so intense that she could not bear the weight of his attention. She looked down, and when she looked up again he had gone back to his work, polishing the rifle barrel so intently that it seemed he might grind it to dust. *Please God preserve him*, Liza thought, and drew the curtains against the impending night.

Chapter Seventeen

Travis did not locate Bone until the sun was nearly down.

The meadow beyond the railway trestle was wide and overgrown with burdocks, nettles, and prairie grass. He had followed twice along the tracks and ranged much deeper before he saw the blue pea coat, like a discarded thing, in a depression where the land sloped to the river.

He moved close enough to get a better look—no closer.

This was Bone. And Bone is dead, Travis thought, or very close. He parted the dried weeds carefully. The alien man lay curled on himself, his long white wrists projecting from the cuffs of the jacket, his shoes so eroded as to be functionless, his watchcap clinging to the bony slope of his scalp. The body was immense, Travis thought, even curled and helpless like this. He was able to see the chest wound, or the evidence of it: a long rust-colored patch running up the pea coat, angry swatches of blood and skin peeking through.

Your own deepest, hidden face. But not this, surely? Surely this was just a broken thing? Pathetic, he thought, but impersonal, like the crushed body of some unfortunate animal.

"Bone," he whispered. "Bone."

There was no response. An eyelid fluttered . . . unless he had imagined it.

Travis moved closer through the brittle weeds. The sunshine was oblique now and did not warm him. "Bone," he said, bending over. "Wake up. Anna sent me. Anna said—"

And Bone's huge fist lashed out.

Travis felt it thump into him, lift him off his feet; felt the astonishing momentum carry him backward.

He sat up slowly.

The fist had struck him squarely on the chest. It might have broken a rib . . . he felt a constriction as he gasped for his breath.

"Bone," he said faintly.

The creature stood up. It loomed, a yard away from him, huge as a gantry tower. The eyes, Travis thought. They were like Anna's—the pupils swollen to fill the sockets—but different, too; colder, somehow; hostile, wary. Bone took one gasping breath and seemed to wince with pain.

Your own deepest, hidden face . . . the words mocked him. Not this, he thought. Not this thing. Wounded, betrayed, hardly human for its wounding and betrayal. . . .

Carefully, Travis stood up.

They faced each other.

"Bone," Travis said.

The creature looked at him.

"Bone, Anna sent me. I'll take you to Anna. I—"

And he stepped forward.

Bone raised his hand. Blue fire licked from his fingertips.

"They hurt you," Travis said. A part of him had long since panicked; he was not sure where the words came from. Somewhere deep inside him. "They hurt you. I know. You trusted them and they hurt you. I know. Let me help." He took a step forward and thought involuntarily of his mother, his

mother who had shamed him, dying and looking at
him with an expression he could only interpret as
reproach. He had hated her then. Her ravaged body
had cried out for his pity and he had withheld it: she
was dying, of course she was dying, dying for her
sins, for the hideous sins she had committed behind
his back. *An old, old bargain*, Travis thought, and
felt a surge of guilt like electricity in him: Christ
God, could he truly have been so cruel?—hating her
when she was dying, hating her *because* she was
dying?

He looked at Bone. Maybe Anna was right.
Maybe this was what he had been then: this dis-
figured thing, suffused with pain so entirely that
there was no room for kindness, trust, thought. Bone
stood, shivering, regarding him from the depths of
his dilated eyes. His fists were clenched and white.

Trembling, Travis reached out toward the monster.

Shortly before dusk Liza Burack answered the timid
knock at the front door and found Faye Wilcox shivering on the veranda. "Why, Faye," she said, and was
suddenly and obscurely afraid: Faye had lost the Baptist Women's election, Faye was here to exact some
strange kind of revenge. . . .

But Faye said, "May I come in?" and it was so
much like a plea, a prayer, that Liza could only nod.

Creath was still in the parlor, the lights off, dusk
thickening about him like a viscous fluid. Liza
steered Faye Wilcox past him and into the kitchen.
Faye sat at the small Formica table, haphazardly
dressed, her hair in loops and tangles down her broad
back, and it was a moment before Liza remembered
to say, "Coffee?"

"No. Thank you."

Liza stood uneasily with her spine against the
kitchen counter. She was conscious of the ticking of
the clock. "Faye . . . if it's about the election. . . ."

"Election?" The Wilcox woman seemed not to understand. "Election—no. It's much more serious than that." She adjusted her smudged bifocals. "Nancy's gone. Did you know that?"

"Nancy? Gone where?"

"Where *he* is, I think. Where Travis is. You know, I pray they both get away safely. Truly, I pray for that. Is it un-Christian, Liza, that I should want them both to leave? But if they stay here they will be hurt. Worse." She looked at Liza directly. "It's tonight, you know."

"I don't understand . . . tonight? You mean the men who are meeting together?"

"Meeting together? Do you believe that's what they're doing? Is that why Creath is cleaning his rifle, Liza?" Faye Wilcox put her plump hands palms downward on the table. Her lips were pursed. "They are a posse. A mob."

Vigilante, Liza thought. But— "You can't know that."

"How could I not? The rumor is all about town. But you don't need a rumor to know."

"But Travis? Surely Travis has left?"

"I believe he has not. Not while Nancy is here."

Liza said nothing, only gripped the beveled edges of the kitchen counter. Faye stood up suddenly. "Your own sister's child! How can you be so hard!"

Travis is lost, she thought dizzily. She had written him out of the book of her heart. But she thought of Creath with his rifle . . . of the other men with theirs. "Faye—"

"No," Faye Wilcox said bleakly. "It was stupid to come here." She went to the kitchen door and opened it. The hinges squealed; a breeze danced inside. There was the smell of woodsmoke. It was what Liza had always loved about autumn, that melancholy perfume on the air, the smell of winter stalking somewhere beyond the horizon. A dry leaf, wind-borne, skirled over the kitchen floor. "Pray for them," Faye said. "Please do at least that much."

Liza swallowed hard and nodded. Faye Wilcox closed the door behind her.

When the time came for Creath to leave the house, the fear Liza felt was for him as much as for Travis: it had lodged in her breast like a living thing. Outside, two big sedans pulled up and sounded their horns. Creath rose from his chair with glacial slowness and went to the door. His rifle was in his hand.

Liza took his arm. "Creath, don't go." He turned to stare at her and she fixed her eyes willfully on his red-checked shirt. His old hunting shirt. "It doesn't matter what they want. Stay. Something bad might happen . . . I don't want you to get hurt."

But he pulled his arm free. The oily metallic smell of the gun was chokingly strong. Liza felt her eyes fill with tears.

"This is bought," Creath said, and she knew at once that he did not mean the gun in his hand but the whole of it, the men waiting outside, the Baptist Women, the tent revival: all this skein of things and people into which she, Liza, had purposefully woven them; and she took a step backward, her breath catching in her throat. "Bought and paid for," Creath said solemnly. "We can't take it back now."

No, Liza thought, it cannot be too late. . . . she thought of Faye Wilcox standing like a funeral stone in the kitchen not an hour ago *(a posse . . . a mob . . . pray for them)* and felt fear close about her like a cloak. Creath had opened the door now, had turned his back; a cold gust of autumn air escorted him toward those two black cars idling in the shadows of the box elders; and she thought *he will die he won't come back again;* she thought *dear God, forgive me* and held out her hand to him, stupidly, imploringly: "Creath—!"

But the cars were pulling away now, engines growling like animals against the night, and Liza faltered on the old boards of the veranda, alone, clutch-

ing her white knit sweater about her throat and
thinking: He was right. This is bought.

Bought and paid for.

Nancy brought the porcelain bowl to Anna's lips.
She drank a little, and the aura of blue fire—it was
constant now—receded a little. "Travis is bringing
Bone here?"

"Travis is attempting to."

Nancy sat back, considering it. The sun was
gone. On cloudless blue days like this, the darkness
came down quickly. The sky beyond the open door
of the switchman's shack was giving up the last of
its glow, and she used the time to light a candle. She
was surprised to find that her hand was trembling.

She turned to Anna. How little there was left of
her! She had faded almost to transparency, her humanity a frail vessel for this blue light that threatened to burst out of her . . . to disperse, Nancy
supposed, like a puff of smoke; and she would be lost
on the wind then, vanished. "Tell me what it's like,"
Nancy said impulsively.

Anna turned her head. "The Jeweled World?"

"Yes."

"A place," Anna said. "I'm sorry . . . I can't describe it in terms you would understand."

"Not like this place," Nancy said.

"No."

"And very beautiful?"

"Often."

"You dream of it?"

"Yes."

"I dream of it sometimes."

"I know," Anna said, her voice far away.

"You must be very powerful . . . to be able to
come here."

"Perhaps too powerful."

She means Bone, Nancy thought. Bone might be
dangerous. "Powerful enough to come here . . .
powerful enough to go back."

"I hope so."

"Did you find what you wanted here?"

And Anna smiled faintly. "I don't know. I think so, yes. A sojourn in the wilderness. You might ask yourself the same question."

"Is that where I am? In the wilderness?" But it was a silly question. She gazed around herself. This shack, the prairie, the night. . . .

"For a long time, I think," Anna said.

We are all exiles. She said, "I envy you . . . I wish I had a place to go back to."

"Here," Anna said.

She held out her hand. Nancy looked dubiously at her.

"It's all I have to give," the alien woman said. "Not much. A little."

Nancy touched her.

She supposed, afterward, that what Anna had given her was a kind of memory, a glimpse into Anna's own past: it was inexpressible, evanescent; all that lingered was the impression of a great light and warmth and vibrant color, as if, Nancy thought, she had penetrated into the heart of the sun. And the memory, inadequate as it was, contained a small heat of its own; it warmed and reassured her.

I will keep this, she thought. I will carry this memory like a charm and only bring it out when I need it.

Anna gazed impassively at her.

"Your world," Nancy said solemnly, "is very strange and beautiful."

Anna smiled. "So is yours."

"Is it?" Nancy looked up, surprised. The candle flickered. Outside this shack a sea of prairie grass bent and hissed in the wind. She said slowly, "It could be. I guess it could be."

But then they heard the first of the gunshots . . . far away but clear and distinct, pinpricks of sound etched against the vastness of the night.

* * *

When they approached the railway trestle both drivers switched off their lights, and the black cars rolled like tumbrils off the main road and across the stubbled meadow, wheels grinding, engines laboring. The railway trestle was black in the moonlight, stone and iron, and Creath fancied he could smell it, a stink of wood and grease and soot-blackened brick. It was hateful.

Bob Clawson sat with his belly up against the steering wheel, dressed, for maybe the first time in his life, in clothes that were less than immaculate: old pants, flannel shirt, threadbare jacket—*and he'll likely burn them in the morning*, Creath thought. Clawson switched off the ignition and the ensuing silence was like a weight. Nobody spoke. There were six men in the car counting himself. Clawson was the leader. Nobody spoke, Creath observed, unless Clawson spoke first, as if they needed his approval. But Greg Morrow sat in the back seat with his daddy's big shotgun on his lap and his eagerness was palpable, a presence in the car; Creath had been aware of it for the last quarter mile, when the only sounds had been the rumble of the engine and the hiss of his own strained breathing. "Everybody out," Clawson said, and it was not much more than a whisper.

They stood in the moonlight with their rifles. Creath felt faintly ridiculous: this army, he thought, this two-bit infantry, half of us scared of the dark. The other car had pulled up ahead; Tim Norbloom was in charge of that little battalion. Creath felt the heft of the rifle in his hand. They had all loaded their weapons during the ride over, and the phrase that ran through Creath's head, idiotically, was *armed and dangerous*. He looked at Greg Morrow, a shadow against the deeper dark . . . he could not be sure, but he believed the boy was grinning. *Armed and dangerous*.

Ahead, Tim Norbloom's crowd had opened the trunk of the other car. Norbloom drew out the torches: lengths of thick pine doweling or spruce two-by-twos wrapped at one end in oily cloth. Norbloom and Clawson's group moved together, made a circle to cut the wind. Norbloom handed out four of the torches—Greg took one; Creath did not. Clawson drew a box of safety matches from his jacket pocket. The torches did not want to take the flame at first, the blackened cotton seeming to resist its own incineration, but then Greg's torch whooshed up all at once, sparking into the night, and he passed on the fire to the others.

There was no hiding now. They had to hurry.

They ran across the meadow toward the railway trestle, Creath lagging behind, his breath laboring. The silence, at first, was eerie; but then Greg Morrow let out a long ululating war whoop that seemed to strike a primitive chord in the other men. The trestle was nearer now, their torches casting a red glow against the black bricks of it, their own shadows huge and manic, and others of them took up Greg's war cry; someone fired a gun into the sky. Echoes bounded back from the trestle arches, and to the men just coming awake in there, Creath thought, it must seem as if a part of hell itself had come to earth among them. They moved sluggishly at first and then more desperately; a pitifully few men to have inspired this army, but that was irrelevant now; now there was no returning. This was bought and paid for. Two hoboes ran shrieking into the cold river, striking out for the other side. Their heads disappeared beneath the black water and Creath could not tell, then, in the flood and panic, whether they survived or were carried away. The vigilantes were laughing, swirling their torches like kids swinging sparklers on Independence Day, but their laughter was not childish . . . or rather, Creath thought dizzily, it was the shrill and hysterical laughter of a child torturing a cat. There was nothing of innocence in it.

He stood still, watching. The gun was a dead thing in his hand. My good Christ, he thought, what if she is here? Seducer, temptress, succubus, the source of his sin: but he knew instantly that he could not raise this rifle to her. And Creath felt a lightness in him then, a feverish buoyancy, as if his feet might spontaneously lift him from this cold fallow ground and deliver him up to some thing or place he could not imagine: death, judgment, the stars. He knew that Bob Clawson was gazing at him, had taken stern note of his immobility, but there was no way to respond, and in truth he no longer cared.

He watched Greg Morrow whirling his torch about his head. The firelight seemed to have transformed him: his grin was maniacal and his eyes feverish. Creath guessed that the boy was paying back some old debt, avenging somehow some irretrievable humiliation. The tramps had mostly fled; the guns had been fired but only into the air; the townsmen had begun to huddle together sheepishly now in the stinking darkness. But Greg was oblivious; possessed, he threw the stub of his torch onto the roof of one of these hovels, oily pasteboard sheets that roared at once into flame. Creath felt his heart skip a beat. The heat washed over him and he thought, *She could be in there.*

Tim Norbloom stepped forward—playing the policeman now—and put a restraining hand on Greg's shoulder. Just then a figure broke from the burning hovel, running for the river: *Anna*, Creath thought for one agonizing moment, but it was not; only a hobo, a dark and half-naked man, possibly a Negro. Creath had begun to relax when he saw Greg raise the rifle and sight along it and pull the trigger. The explosion in this confined space beneath the trestle was deafening. Creath winced, and when he opened his eyes he saw the tramp, dead or mortally wounded, spreadeagled on the ground. The light of the burning hovel danced on his skin. He might have been bleeding; in this light everything was bloody.

It changes things, Creath thought. They had come here prepared to kill. But, in the event, they had backed away from it. And it was Greg's fault mainly: he had misled them, there was no threat in this pathetic slum. Creath saw Tim Norbloom eyeing the boy with frank contempt. Some of the men cursed. The enormity of this was too great; they felt too much like murderers. You, too, Tim Norbloom, Creath thought: that guilt is palpable. In this strange hour his mind was quite lucid and Creath imagined he could read other men's thoughts. There was a kind of skewed victory in it despite the dead man on the ground, because *she* had not been here . . . Anna was still alive, and a part of him exalted at the thought.

The men walked back to the cars. The night had soured on them. Creath, his ears still ringing with the proximity of the gunshots, watched Bob Clawson remonstrating with Greg Morrow, saw the boy's impassioned response; Clawson went to Norbloom then and the two of them spoke heatedly. Creath heard the sound but could not make sense of it. The trestle was eerily lit by the embers of the Hoovertown and a freight train came highballing out of the east, oblivious.

Clawson and Norbloom were arguing. Norbloom turned away, his fists clenched, and climbed into the second of the two automobiles. The two parties broke up, and Creath watched Norbloom's sedan bouncing over the rutted soil. Clawson sat at the wheel of his own car stonily; his cheeks were flushed pink. Creath climbed in last. "Thank God it's at least over," he said.

Clawson looked back at Greg. Greg stared at him.

"We're not done yet," Clawson said grimly. "Norbloom is an idiot. It's important to finish this. We have begun it and we are obliged to finish it."

"One more place," Greg said evenly. "I'll show you the way."

Please God, no, Creath thought, and Bob Clawson revved the motor.

Travis saw the trestle fire from a distance and circled to the south, keeping to a line of windbreak trees. White smoke curled up in the moonlight and the cold wind carried the hoarse shouting of the men across the prairie.

Bone was frightened. Travis could tell. He crouched in a drainage ditch and the alien crouched beside him. The alien must be tremendously strong, Travis thought, to have come even this far. His jacket was a mass of blood and there was fresh blood welling up now, a brighter red in the moonlight. An ordinary man would have died. But Bone was not ordinary, not a man. Bone's eyes were fixed on the trestle and the flicker of fires there.

"You've seen this kind of thing before," Travis said.

Bone did not respond, only stared. Travis took it for a kind of assent.

They crouched, hidden, and listened to the snap of gunshots. Travis glanced periodically at Bone, who seemed wreathed with a fire of his own, a flickering aura; but it cast no shadows in the darkness beneath the trees and Travis guessed another man might see nothing at all. When the shouting died away and the gunshots ceased Travis and Bone moved closer, Travis imbued with a sense of deep foreboding: now there had been violence, now some invisible border had been passed.

The hobo jungle was in embers. There was no one left here . . . only the body of a black man Travis had known very slightly, Harley was his name; Harley was dead from a gunshot wound to the back. Travis knelt over the body. He could not bring himself to touch it: a revulsion, not at death, but at his own utter helplessness. I knew this man, he thought.

Bone watched him kneeling . . . and after a moment Bone extended his arm and touched him.

Visions ran like a river between them. Travis fell back under the assault of the projected memories. This was Bone, he thought dazedly: Bone had seen too many places like this, an ocean of them; had seen men burned, beaten, trampled under foot. The cavalcade of images was stunning, faces and bodies like schools of fish. Travis gazed up in awe at that pale skull of a face. He is the ultimate exile, he thought, king of exiles; and he felt all the fists that had pummeled him, all the blows and curses; saw Deacon and Archie bent over him, then Deacon with a pistol in his hand and Archie dead beside him; he saw the railroad cops gather about Bone in a ring and felt what Bone had felt as he struck out and sent them whirling into the chaos that separates spacetime from spacetime. . . .

"Christ Almighty," Travis whispered. "You can do that? You can really do that?"

Bone stood erect. His aura deepened. His eyes were squeezed shut, his face disguised beneath his own cold illumination. Sweet Jesus, Travis thought, he *could* be me: the lines of his face rippled like a reflection in deep water. Travis turned away, gasping. So little of humanity left in this creature. . . .

Your own deepest, hidden face. Was that possible? Maybe so: Bone and the Pale Woman both inside him, Janus-faced, calling over the gaps and chasms of him toward some unimaginable union—

But that made him think of Anna, and of Nancy, and of where the vigilantes might have gone from here. He made himself stand up. "Bone, follow me," he said.

Bone stepped forward and stumbled. The leg wound, Travis thought: this tremendous energy faltering, the human fraction of him too close to death.

No longer as frightened as he was, Travis put his arm around the alien and the two of them loped eastward, ludicrous in the moonlight, along the frozen bank of the river.

Chapter Eighteen

The interior of the switchman's shack was full of radiance, the human parts of Anna hidden beneath this amorphous glow. What remained of the alien woman's human disguise was so diminished—though still in its fragile way beautiful—that Nancy felt frightened. She thought: in a way I *am* in the wilderness. The wilderness was where you confronted the basic things, Nancy thought, life and death, and here she was, approaching a strange wasteland, face-to-face with Anna's transformation. There had been nothing in her life to prepare her for this. She was out here all by herself. Out here in the wilderness.

Travis must be near, she thought. Travis and Bone. She risked a glance at Anna—that inhumanly white body in its nexus of glow—and shivered. Maybe Travis had been right all along, there was nothing human in the motivation of these creatures; maybe she had been used . . . and, used, would be discarded. There wasn't Anna's liquid voice to reassure her now. Only a kind of faith. Faith and kinship.

The night was very dark. Please Travis, she thought, please hurry up.

Outside, in the darkness, an automobile engine murmured and stopped . . . a door slammed shut. Nancy gasped at the sound of it.

"Anna! Anna, wake up, somebody's here—!"

Anna's eyes sprang open, but the pupils had eclipsed the whites; blue fire seemed to coalesce into fibrous wings behind her, and she showed no sign of human comprehension.

As they moved along the riverbank Travis supported the alien man's weight, which was negligible.

He must be hollow-boned, Travis thought, like a bird. But he guessed it was only the shedding of this human skin. The strange light burned brightly about him, and Travis, touching him, was strangely affected by it; the night had come alive with phantom shapes and colors. He sensed dizzily the truth of what Anna had told him: there were worlds within worlds, kinds and shapes of worlds which coexisted with this one, infinitely layered and infinitely complex. He concentrated on following the riverbank by starlight, step by step, frightened that he might lose his way. A misstep, Travis thought, and we could tumble off the Earth altogether.

Bone was dying or coming to life—as much one thing as the other, so far as Travis could tell. Certainly this physical part of him was very weak. Bone could not have come this distance without Travis's help. But the alien part of Bone seemed to be growing steadily stronger, as if the proximity to Anna were feeding him . . . we must be a beacon light, Travis thought, down here along the riverbed. Thin shales of ice had formed in the hollows of the ground, and Travis saw his own reflection in them and Bone's, luminous against the starry sky and almost too strange to bear. In some way, he thought, Bone had become very powerful indeed.

"Just a little farther," Travis said. He was not sure the alien understood him. It was a reassurance as much for himself as for Bone. "Just a little farther now." The place where Bone had struck him was throbbing and it pained him when he breathed; Bone lurched against him and Travis bit his lip to keep from crying out. One step at a time, he thought. Steady.

In some way, Travis thought, he *is* me. Ugly, outcast, betrayed. That ravaged face, these wounds. And I am bearing him toward a healing I cannot share. For me no Pale Woman. . . . But there was no such creature, Anna had said, among humankind; Anna herself was a freak, a kind of monster, as Bone was a monster; human beings, she had said, carried such monsters inside themselves always, estranged or buried, despised and unforgiven. . . .

Walk, he thought. Just walk. The brittle reeds snapped beneath his feet. He looked up, and the stars seemed to dance about him like fireflies. But then, he thought, some conciliation *is* possible, must be: himself finding and forgiving himself, chasms mended, old wounds healed—

Just walk, he thought.

Landmarks were difficult to follow in this light. He recognized the steeple of the train station and then, it seemed only a moment later, the stand of box elders surrounding the meadow where the switchman's shack stood. "Up here," he told Bone. "Up the riverbank. I guess we made it."

Travis scrabbled up the hard-packed mud with Bone beside him. So close now, he thought. So close. But at the top of the river's gentle slope he paused.

The moon had set, but in the starlight—and a gentler illumination that seemed to emanate from Bone, from the shack, from the meadow itself—he was able to see the black sedan parked in the dark of the trees and the men who climbed out of it.

"Bone," he said tentatively—

But Bone stood straight up, his weakness and his humanity both blasted away in a sudden and apocalyptic burst of blue light; across the meadow six figures approached the switchman's shack and Bone, watching them, roared out his pain and indignation.

He had seen them before. He knew what they were. Bone flew across the meadow on a

*whirlwind of strange energies, his humanity
fading like firefly light: These were killers,
murderers, the same cruel species he had seen
so often in the railyards; but now the Other
was close, he must not let them threaten her.
This new part of him, not human, was hugely
strong, and Bone abandoned himself to it.*

*They were his enemies. They would fall.
He felt the lightless flames that danced at his
fingertips and thought: They must.*

It was his last human thought.

Creath, climbing out of the car in the silent
meadow, felt his legs begin to buckle beneath him. It
was dark here, past midnight now, the possibility of
murder all too imminent: it was written in these
men, in their grim intensity. Maybe they were not
murderers by nature—if there was such a thing—but
they had sundered, this night, all their daylight inhi-
bitions. This was their Halloween, their bac-
chanalia. And Clawson was no longer the focus;
Clawson had subtly deferred to Greg Morrow, who
more precisely embodied the spirit of the adventure.
It was Greg who had committed the boldest trans-
gression. It was Greg who had murdered a man.

"Quiet now," Greg Morrow said as the five men
formed up behind him. Only rifles tonight, no
torches. "They are out here. I'm sure of it."

"Fornicators and adulterers," Clawson said, as if
to reassure himself.

"Worse than that," Greg murmured. And periodically he turned his eyes toward Creath, as if to
say: I did not plan this. Some wild trajectory has carried us all here. But it is right and just and—Creath
saw this in his eyes—a fitting culmination.

Greg Morrow, Creath saw, was not wholly sane.
But, he thought, Christ, which of us is? Which of us
out here in the darkness?

They crept through the trees. Creath felt his
own cold sweat breaking out on his forehead. He

shivered with it. There was frost on everything, a starry glittering. Winter cutting close. And he thought: well, what if she *is* here? What then?

There was no answer in him. He felt the heft of the rifle in his hand. But all these other men had rifles, too.

Greg bulled ahead to this pathetic tumbledown shack, the place where the half-crazed railway switchman Colliuto had lived until some kids found him dead of exposure back in the spring of '25. The years and the weather had not been kind to the place. Slat walls, tar-paper roof, a hole up top, where a stovepipe might once have exited, plugged now with a bird's nest of hard mud and prairie grass. Cold and filthy inside there, Creath thought. Surely it could not be occupied—but a faint light leaked through the wallboards.

Greg, with that crazy flushed grin fixed in place, kicked through the door. It fell away like pasteboard before him. Dust billowed up. The men pressed closer and then, in the eerie blue light, fell back.

Creath felt his neck hairs standing erect.

The thing in there craned its head to gaze at him. A lifetime of religious fears made him step away in deference. These other men shrieked out their dismay . . . but it is only the natural culmination, Creath thought wildly, the reasonable consequence: we are beyond the pale now, now we consort with demons and angels.

In truth, he could not say which this was. Clearly the creature was not human. It stood up within the confines of the shack, and Creath was aware of its luminous wings—if they were wings—spread out behind it, peacock vortices of light without substance. And he peered into that face.

He would have thought there was no capacity for shock left him, but his eyes widened in stunned recognition.

It was her.

His limbs felt cold and distant as ice. Demon or angel, he thought, it was her, sweet God, his secret love, loved and hated and stolen from him: he moved his mouth: *Anna*—

And she came forward.

The other men fled back toward the automobile. "Christ, look there," Bob Clawson was shouting, "another of the damned monsters—on the riverbank!" Creath saw it then, too, hurtling toward them across the meadow, a similar creature. He could feel its anger even at this distance. The car's motor roared. Now only the two of them were left here, Creath and Greg, equally immobile, staring and helpless. Because, Creath thought, in some way we have always expected this. We have earned it. His thoughts moved with a high, wild lucidity. *This is bought and paid for.*

The Wilcox girl, Nancy, broke from the shack and ran for the riverbank, her arms pinwheeling.

The angel looked at Creath with Anna's face, inscrutable.

The demon hurtled toward him.

Creath turned in a kind of graceless slow motion and saw Greg Morrow raise his rifle.

"Bone," Travis said faintly. But there was no calling him back.

Travis fell to his hands and knees in the frozen meadow. It was all happening too fast for him. Bone fled across the meadow like the ghost of his own rages and fears at last set loose: he will kill them all, Travis thought, God help us, and he thought about Nancy.

But she had broken free from the shack and was moving toward him. Unmindful of his own pain, he stood and ran to her. She came into his arms but he could not look away; he saw Bone—all light and fire and pain—converging on the townsmen, who scattered before him. Nancy seemed to want to burrow into him, but he pushed her back: "Listen," he said, "we have to get away. Bone's crazy, he's full of hatred—everything he learned here is hatred—and we have to get away from him."

"No," Nancy said. "Anna promised—"

"She didn't promise anything! This is dangerous, this has always been dangerous! Nancy—" He tugged at her, "Come on—"

We can move down and away along the river-bank, Travis thought. That would be good. That might afford them some safety. But he did not see Greg Morrow aiming his rifle across the empty meadow and he could only be helplessly surprised at the sound of it, at the pain of the bullet as it passed through his shoulder.

The crack of the rifle broke his trance. Greg had fired and missed the demon thing, but seemed unaware of it; Creath watched the boy's supernatural steadiness as he swung the weapon toward the switchman's shack.

The demon was almost on them and Creath was able to hear the sound it made, an eerie and inhuman wailing, a howl compressed of all the sorrow and indignity of the world. It chilled him. The thing must be able to see, Creath thought, must know that it could not reach Greg Morrow before he committed the act he was so obviously contemplating. The boy swung up the rifle barrel toward the thing in the shack—the Anna-thing.

How beautiful she still was. Strange that he could admit it even to himself (and there seemed plenty of time for admissions in this new lucidity of his, everything moving at quarterspeed): It should be loathsome, the way she had changed. But she was not loathsome. Merely delicate, fragile, embedded in light, wrapped round with amber and turquoise light, winged with light; the beauty in it was ethereal, beyond lust, heartbreaking; it spoke—as it had always, he guessed, spoken—to his deepest nugget of self. He thought of things lost, time lost, opportunities lost, whole lives lost in the living of a life. Tears sprang to his eyes. I am too old to cry, he thought. Too old and too weary and too close to death. Death wheeling toward him on an autumn wind, shimmering.

It was this beauty that Greg must hate, he thought, and saw the boy targeting his rifle on her.

Creath sighed. Death so close but not close enough to save her. He imagined he could see the boy's finger tightening on the trigger.

His own gun flew up. He was hardly conscious of it. The recoil bucked it into his shoulder. Creath cried out with the pain.

Greg Morrow spun away. The bullet had taken him cleanly. He was dead at once. His rifle fired—the reflexive closing of the fingers—but the bullet went wild.

Creath felt his own rifle drop to the ground.

Anna was alive yet. She turned her eyes on him, round inscrutable wells.

That was good, Creath thought, that she would live. This at least.

The demon fell on Greg Morrow's body, appeared to pick it up and fling it—but this made no sense—in a direction that was not any perceptible direction; the body simply disappeared. Creath looked at the demon calmly and saw a face there, indistinct but full of rage; and that, too, he thought, was good and proper, that death should have a face.

Creath turned to confront the creature, openhanded.

Death came on him like a flaming sword.

"Go on," Travis told Nancy. "Down the riverbank. Hide."

She didn't want to leave him, but she glanced at the figure of Bone—Bone transformed—and retreated sobbing from the meadow.

Travis could not move. The pain of the bullet wound had radiated through him. All the fatigue of

these last few days had come down on him all at
once, like sleep. His eyelids were heavy. Strange, he
thought, to be on the edge of death and only feel this
weariness.

On his back in the icy meadow, Travis turned
his head.

The automobile had gone. Bone moved in on the
two men remaining—Greg and Creath: he recognized their silhouettes in the moonlight—and then
Creath raised his rifle (it all happened too quickly to
follow); then Bone was on them and they were gone,
tossed into that limbo between worlds, discarded.
Dead.

Bone turned back toward him.

Travis lay helplessly, watching as the monster
approached him.

There was nothing of Bone left in this thing. It
was made of light but it was not without substance.
Its footsteps pressed into the prairie grass. It smelled
of ozone and burning leaves, and Travis did not suppose it could support itself long in this world: it con-
tradicted too many of the natural laws. You could
tell by looking. Such a thing ought not to exist.

The rage and pain of it were still perceptible. It
had a purpose, Travis sensed, and the purpose was to
protect the Anna-thing long enough for their cou-
pling to take place; it was hostile to every threat.
And it knew him.

The monster hovered over him.

Your own deepest, hidden face.

Betrayed, he thought, deceived, yes, striking out
now, unbound, no victims left but himself. But if
this *was* himself then he could no longer deny it. He
gazed without fear into those fiery eyes. The self
submitting to the verdict of the self. Christ knows
he had done it to others. Had turned on his dying
mother, had turned on Nancy when she needed him;
now himself: it was only logical. "Kill me," he whispered. "Kill me then, if that's what you've come to
do."

But the creature turned away. It went to the shack; the meadow was suddenly, prosaically empty. Travis gaped up at the stars.

Nancy ran to him, weeping.

She staunched his wound and made a sort of pillow of prairie grass for him. She took off her own cloth coat and laid it over him.

The night was cold, and Travis was grateful.

Chapter Nineteen

Through what remained of the night she kept him warm. Travis was intermittently lucid. He imagined he could see the stars wheeling overhead. When the dawn came he said, "Are they in there?"

"In the shack? Yes."

He sat up, though the effort was murderous. Nancy said, "You need a doctor."

He shook his head. He wasn't bleeding anymore and he could move his arm. It was a clean wound and might not infect. "I need to get warm. I need food."

"We could build a fire . . . but it might draw somebody's attention."

"Build it," Travis said. "There won't be anybody coming out here today."

He warmed himself at the fire. He still did not trust himself to walk. Dizziness came and went, and nausea. Nancy brought him water from the river. But she knew he needed to eat, too.

"There's some food left in the shack," Nancy said.

"I wonder how long it takes."

"Don't know. She never said." It was unimaginable, the prodigies of healing that must be going on in there. She had seen Bone and she knew Anna and she could not conceive of a single creature emerging from that marriage of fire and water, earth and air.

Travis looked at her. "You know, we can't go back."

"I know."

"There's nowhere much we can go."

"I thought maybe west. California, maybe." She shrugged. "It's warmer."

He nodded.

Nancy said, "You mean it?"

"What?"

"About traveling together?"

"Yes . . . I mean, if you're willing."

She gazed at him as if from a distance. "What did you see out there with Bone? What did he show you?"

Travis shrugged.

They appeared, Anna and Bone, briefly, at noon.

The sunlight made everything prosaic. The air was still cool but the autumn sun beat down with real pressure. Everything was outlined in it, Nancy thought, each stalk of grass, the grain elevators black on the horizon, a sparrow swooping across the meadow. There were dust motes everywhere.

They emerged from the switchman's shack, a single being now. She could see none of Bone or Anna in this creature. She was reminded instead of a sort of bird—those structureless wings of light behind it, a graceful arch that suggested a body, swirls of darkness for eyes. It did not fly but hung suspended in the air, buoyant. She held her breath. The creature was difficult to look at and seemed to possess too many angles, as if a stained-glass church window had been folded and folded on itself, the delicate rose and amber light caught up in labyrinths the eye could not trace. It moved toward Travis.

Nancy thought he might struggle to his feet, even injured as he was; might run away. But he did not. The creature advanced on him and he only looked at it, his eyes wide and fearless.

Dear God, Nancy thought, what *did* he learn out there?

The creature hovered. She saw one wing come down. Its membrane of light moved across Travis—or through him—like a caress. The gesture was at once so tender and so entirely alien that Nancy felt a tingling at her neck. Then the creature moved away, rose up or diminished; she could not say which.

She went to Travis. With an expression of slow wonder he peeled away the bandage Nancy had made for him.

The wound was closed; there was only the hint of a scar.

"They know us," he told her, hoarse with awe. "They know us yet."

And then they were alone. The creature that was Anna and Bone moved away across the meadow in an impossible motion that made her blink and avert her eyes. Gone, she thought, vanished into the lanes and pathless alleys between the worlds . . . and for a moment she was stricken with an inexpressible longing. Her memory of the Jeweled World was strong in her and she thought, I want to follow, follow . . . but Bone and Anna were gone where there was no following, vanished along some invisible axis. There was only the prairie—prairie grass, buckbrush, dry foxtail and lupine running in swells to a distant shore of sky; summer and winter, spring and fall contained in it (somehow) all at once—and Nancy thought: why, I guess it is enough. It *is* enough.

She moved with trepidation into the dark hollow of the vacant shack. It seemed now as if she had lived much of her life in this confined space—made alien, curiously, by Anna's absence. The door had fallen away when Greg Morrow kicked it. Fingers of sunlight probed into all the secret places. The mattress was tawdry and stained, Anna's old clothes in a heap on it, and Bone's there, too, his old blue pea coat—bloodstained—discarded in a corner.

She folded the dress neatly and put it aside. It was a small gesture but soothing. The blue pea coat was heavy with blood but deserved, she thought, the same act of respect. But when she lifted it in her hand a bundle dropped from one of its pockets.

Nancy, curious, reached for it.

Coda

The freight car they rode out of Haute Montagne was crowded, and Nancy was dismayed by the people who filled it. These were not just hoboes like the men she had seen under the railway trestle but whole families, men and women and children, migrating westward with winter and poverty hard behind them. Outcasts, she thought, exiles, and how easily we might have joined them, become indistinguishable from them. . . . In truth, she thought, we are not much better off, despite the money that had fallen from Bone's pea coat (enough to buy food, pay a little rent)—but, too, she thought, in some way we *are* different. It was written in Travis's face.

The granaries and the water tower fell away behind them. A cold wind came through the slats in the freight car and made her press into Travis's shoulder. He held her with a gentleness she had not sensed in him before. She looked at his face and he was frowning into the gray distance, worried, she guessed, about where they were going and what they would do there; but there was a second quality in him that was unfamiliar, utterly new. He sensed her attention and smiled at her. And it was the smile, Nancy thought wonderingly, of a man who has just forgiven someone, or who has been, himself, forgiven.

* * *

There were no funeral services held in Haute Montagne in the month of November. No one would say (though some suspected) that Creath Burack was dead. Liza lit a candle in the parlor window each night all that cold month in the hope that her husband might find his way home. But he did not, and come the first snow Liza laid away the candlestick in a bureau drawer, secure between a lavender sachet and a neatly folded linen tablecloth. For him, as for her, there was no returning.

A Special Preview of
THE DIVIDE
the new Science Fiction novel by
Robert Charles Wilson

Imagine losing your personality . . . feeling it slip
and alter, steadily changing, until the person living
in your body is no longer recognizable as *you*. Imagine being able to understand what is happening, but
powerless to stop it. Imagine . . . and you will understand the feelings of John Shaw. The Divide is his
story.

Shaw was a "designed" child—the product of a clandestine research project meant to create a superior
human being. But when government funding ran
out, Shaw not only lost the only father he had ever
known—researcher Max Kyriakides—but was left without the monitoring his altered body required. Now,
years later, he is a grown man . . . but a man whose
mind is not entirely his own. . . .

Such an ordinary house. Such an ordinary beginning.

But I *want* it to be an ordinary house, Susan Christopher thought. An ordinary house with an ordinary man in it. Not this monster—to whom I must deliver a message.

It was a yellow brick boarding house in the St. Jamestown area of Toronto, a neighborhood of low-rent high-rises and immigrant housing. Susan was from suburban Los Angeles—lately from the University of Chicago—and she felt misplaced here. She stood a moment in the chill, sunny silence of the afternoon, double-checking the address Dr. Kyriakides had written on a slip of pink memo paper. This number, yes, this street.

She fought a momentary urge to run away.

Then up the walk through a scatter of October leaves, pause a moment in the cold foyer . . . the inner door stood open . . . finally down a corridor to the door marked with a chipped gilt number 2.

She knocked twice, aware of her small knuckles against the ancient veneer of the door. Across the hall, a wizened East Indian man peered out from behind his chain lock. Susan looked up at the ceiling, where a swastika had been spray-painted onto the cloudy stucco. She was about to knock again when the door opened under her hand.

But it was a woman who answered . . . a young woman in a white blouse, denim skirt, torn khaki jacket. Her feet were bare on the cracked linoleum. The woman's expression was sullen—her lips in a ready, belligerent pout—and Susan dropped her eyes from the narrow face to the jacket, where there was a small constellation of buttons and badges: BON JOVI, JIM MORRISON, LED ZEPPELIN. . . .

"You want something?"

Susan guessed this was a French Canadian accent, the nasality and the dropped "th" sound. She forced herself to meet the woman's eyes. Woman or girl? Maybe nineteen or twenty years old: a few years younger than I am, Susan thought, therefore "girl" —but it was hard to be sure, with the makeup and all.

She cleared her throat. "I'm looking for John Shaw."

"Oh . . . *him*."

"Is he here?"

"No." The girl ran a hand through her hair. Long nails. Short hair.

"But he lives here?"

"Uh—sometimes. Are you a friend of his?"

Susan shook her head. "Not exactly . . . are you?"

Now there was the barest hint of a smile. "Not exactly." The girl extended her hand. "I'm Amelie."

The hand was small and cool. Susan introduced herself; Amelie said, "He's not here . . . but you can maybe find him at the 24-Hour on Wellesley. You know, the doughnut shop?"

Susan nodded. She would look for "Wellesley" on her map.

Amelie said, "Is it important? You look kind of, ah, worried."

"It's pretty important," Susan said, thinking: *Life or death*: Dr. Kyriakides had told her that.

Susan saw him for the first time, her first real look at him, through the plate-glass window of the doughnut shop.

She allowed herself this moment, seeing him without being seen. She recognized him from the pictures Dr. Kyriakides had shown her. But Susan imagined she might have guessed who he was, just from looking at him—that she would have known, at least, that he was not entirely normal.

To begin with, he was alone.

He sat at a small table in the long room, three steps down from the sidewalk. His face was angled up at the October sunlight, relishing it. There was a chessboard in front of him—the board built into the lacquered surface of the table and the pieces arranged in ready ranks.

She had dreamed about this, about meeting him, dreams that occasionally bordered on nightmares. In the dreams John Shaw was barely human, his head unnaturally enlarged, his eyes needle-sharp and unblinking. The real John Shaw was nothing like that, of course, in his photographs or here, in the flesh; his monstrosities, she thought, were buried—but she mustn't think of him that way. He was in trouble and he needed her help.

Hello, John Shaw, she thought.

His hair was cut close, a burr cut, but that was fashionable now; he was meticulously clean-shaven. Regular features, frown lines, maps of character emerging from the geography of his fairly young face. Here is a man, Susan thought, who worries a lot. A gust of wind lifted her hair; she reached up to smooth it back and he must have glimpsed the motion; his head turned—a swift owlish flick of the eyes, and for that moment he did *not* seem human; the swivel of his head was too calculated, the focus of his eyes too fine. His eyes, suddenly, were like the eyes in her dreams. John Shaw regarded her through the window and she felt spotlit, or, worse, *pinned*—a butterfly in a specimen case.

Both of them were motionless in this tableau until, finally, John Shaw raised a hand and beckoned her inside.

Well, Susan Christopher thought, there's no turning back now, is there?

Breathing hard, she moved down the three cracked steps and through the door of the shop. There was no one inside but John Shaw and the middle-aged woman refilling the coffee machine. Susan approached him and then stood mute beside the table: she couldn't find the words to begin.

He said, "You might as well sit down."

His voice was controlled, unafraid, neutral in accent. Susan took the chair opposite him. They were separated, now, by the ranks of the chessboard.

He said, "Do you play?"

"Oh . . . I didn't come here to play chess."

"No. Max sent you."

Her eyes widened at this Holmes-like deduction. John said, "Well, obviously you were looking for me. And I've taken some pains to be unlooked-for. I could imagine the American government wanting a word with me. But you don't look like you work for the government. It wasn't a long shot—I'm assuming I'm correct?"

"Yes," Susan stammered. "Dr. Kyriakides . . . yes."

"I thought he might do this. Sometime."

"It's more important than you think." But how to *say* this? "He wants you to know—"

John hushed her. "Humor me," he said. "Give me a game."

She looked at the board. In high school, she had belonged to the chess club. She had even played in a couple of local tournaments—not too badly. But—

"You'll win," she said.

"You know that about me?"

"Dr. Kyriakides said—"

"Your move," John said.

She advanced the white king's pawn two squares, reflexively.

"No talk," John instructed her. "As a favor." He responded with his own king's pawn. "I appreciate it."

She played out the opening—a Ruy Lopez—but was soon in a kind of free fall; he did something unexpected with his queen's knight and her pawn ranks began to unravel. His queen stood in place, a vast but nonspecific threat; he gave up a bishop to expose her king and the queen at last came swooping out to give checkmate. They had not even castled.

Of course, the winning was inevitable. She knew—Dr. Kyriakides had told her—that John Shaw had played tournament chess for a time; that he had never lost a game; that he had dropped out of competition before his record and rating began to attract attention. She wondered how the board must look to him. Simple, she imagined. A graph of possibilities; a kindergarten problem.

He thanked her and began to set up the pieces again, his large hands moving slowly, meticulously. She said, "You spend a lot of time here?"

"Yes."

"Playing chess?"

"Sometimes. Most of the regulars have given up on me."

"But you still do it."

"When I get the chance."

"But surely . . . I mean, don't you always win?"

He looked at her. He smiled, but the smile was cryptic . . . she couldn't tell whether he was amused or disappointed.

"One hopes," John Shaw said.

She walked back with him to the rooming house, attentive now, her fears beginning to abate, but still reluctant: how could she tell him? But she must.

She used this time to observe him. What Dr.

Kyriakides had told her was true: John wore his strangeness like a badge. There was no pinning down exactly what it was that made him different. His walk was a little ungainly; he was too tall; his eyes moved restlessly when he spoke. But none of that added up to anything significant. The real difference, she thought, was more subtle. Pheromones, or something on that level. She imagined that if he sat next to you on a bus you would notice him immediately—turn, look, maybe move to another seat. No reason, just this uneasiness. Something *odd* here.

It was almost dark, an early October dusk. The street lights blinked on, casting complex shadows through the brittle trees. Coming up the porch stairs to the boarding house Susan saw him hesitate, stiffen a moment, lock one hand in a fierce embrace of the banister. My God, she thought, it's some kind of seizure—he's sick—but it abated as quickly as it had come. He straightened and put his key in the door.

Susan said, "Will Amelie be here?"

"Amelie works a night shift at a restaurant on Yonge Street. She's out by six most evenings."

"You live with her?"

"No. I don't live with her."

The apartment seemed even more debased, in this light, than Susan had guessed from her earlier glimpse of it. It was one room abutting a closet-sized bedroom—she could make out the jumbled bedclothes through the door—and an even tinier kitchen. The room smelled greasy: Amelie's dinner, Susan guessed, leftovers still congealing in the pan. Salvation Army furniture and a sad, dim floral wallpaper. Why would he live here? Why not a mansion—a palace? He could have had that. But he was sick, too . . . maybe that had something to do with it.

She said, "I know what you are."

He nodded mildly, as if to say, *Yes, all right*. He

shifted a stack of magazines to make room for himself on the sofa. "You're one of Max's students?"

"I was," she corrected. "Molecular biology. I took a sabbatical."

"Money?"

"Money mostly. My father died after a long illness. It was expensive. There was the possibility of loans and so forth, but I didn't feel—I just didn't enjoy the work anymore. Dr. Kyriakides offered me a job until I was ready to face my thesis again. At first I was just collating notes, you know, doing some library research for a book he's working on. Then—"

"Then he told you about me."

"Yes."

"He must trust you."

"I suppose so."

"I'm sure of it. And he sent you here?"

"Finally, yes. He wasn't sure you'd be willing to talk directly to him. But it's very important."

"Not just *auld lang syne?*"

"He wants to see you."

"For medical reasons?"

"Yes."

"Am I ill, then?"

"Yes."

He smiled again. The smile was devastating— superior, knowing, but at the same time obviously forced, an act of bravery. He said, "Well, I thought so."

They talked for a long time.

Dr. Kyriakides had already told her some of this. He had kept tabs on John, but surreptitiously, since it was a violation of his funding agreements to do so . . . and he had no illusions about the source of his grants. Susan was able to anticipate some of what John told her. But some of it was new.

He said, "It depends on what you call a symptom, doesn't it?"

The research project ended when John was five years old. He was adopted out to a childless couple, the Woodwards, a middle-income family living in a bleak Chicago suburb. The Woodwards renamed him Benjamin, though he continued to think of himself as John. From the beginning, his adoptive parents were disturbed by his uniqueness. He didn't always do especially well in school—he was contemptuous of his teachers and sometimes a discipline problem—but he read beyond his years and he made conversation like an adult . . . which, the Woodwards told him, was very disrespectful.

"Jim Woodward was a lathe operator at an aerospace plant and he resented my intelligence. Obviously, a child doesn't know this, or doesn't want to admit it. I labored for eight years under the impression that I was doing something terribly wrong—that he hated me for some fundamental, legitimate reason. And so I worked hard to please him. I tried to impress him. For example, I learned to play the flute in junior high. Borrowed a school instrument and some books. I taught myself. He loved Vivaldi: he had this old Heathkit stereo he had cobbled together out of a kit and he would play Vivaldi for hours—it was the only time I saw anything like rapture on his face. And so I taught myself the Concerto in G, the passages for flute. And when I had it down, I played it for him. Not just the notes. I went beyond that. I *interpreted* it. He sat there listening, and at first I thought he was in shock—he had that dumbfounded expression. I mistook it for pleasure. I played harder. And he just sat there until I was finished. I thought I'd done it, you see, that I'd communicated with him, that he would approve of me now. And then I put the flute back in the case and looked at him. And he blinked a couple of times, and then he said, 'I bet you think you're pretty fucking good, don't you?' "

"That's terrible," Susan said.

"But I wasn't convinced. It just wasn't good enough, that's all. So I thought, well, what else is there that matters to him?

"He had a woodworking shop in the basement. We were that kind of family, the Formica counters in the kitchen, Sunday at the Presbyterian church every once in a while, the neighbors coming over to play bridge and the woodwork shop downstairs. But he had quality tools, Dremel and Black & Decker and so on, and he took a tremendous amount of pride in the work he did. He built a guitar once, some cousin paid him a hundred dollars for it, and he must have put in three times that in raw materials, and when it was finished it was a work of art, bookmatched hardwood, polished and veneered—it took him months. When I saw it, I wanted it. But it had been bought and paid for, and he had to send it away. I wanted him to make another one, but he was already involved in some other project, and that was when I saw my opportunity—I said, '*I'll* build it.'

"I was twelve years old. I had never so much as touched his woodworking tools. 'Show me,' I said. He said, 'You'll never manage it. It's not a beginner's project.' I said, 'Let me try.' And I think now he saw it as *his* big opportunity . . . maybe this would teach me a lesson. So he agreed. He showed me how to work the tools and he gave me some books on luthiery. He even took me to lumberyards, helped me pick out decent woods."

John paused to sip his cappucino. "I worked on the guitar that summer whenever he was out of the house. Because it was an experiment—you understand? This would be the communication, he would see this and love me for doing it, and if he didn't—all bets were off. So I took it very seriously. I cut and sanded, I routed the neck, I installed the fretwire and the tuning machinery. I was possessed by that guitar. There was not a weekday afternoon through July or August I was out of the house. I was dizzy with lacquer fumes half the time. And when he came home I would hide the project . . . I didn't want him to see it until it was ready. I cleaned the tools and the workshop every day; I was meticulous. I think he forgot about it. Thought I'd given up. Until I showed it to him."

Susan said, "Oh, no."

"It was perfect, of course. Max probably told you what his research had suggested, long before it was fashionable science—that the neocortical functions aren't just 'intelligence.' It's also dexterity, timing, the attention span, the sense of pitch, eye-hand coordination—things as pertinent to music or luthiery as they are to, say, mathematics. Jim Woodward thought he'd found a task that was beyond me. In fact, he could hardly have picked one I was better suited to. Maybe that guitar wasn't flawless, but it was close. It was a work of art."

Susan said, "He hated it."

John smiled his humorless, raw smile. "He took it personally. I showed him the guitar. The last varnish was barely dry. I strummed a G chord. I handed it to him . . . the final evidence that I was worthy of him. To him it must have been, I don't know, a slap in the face, a gesture of contempt. He took the guitar, checked it out. He sighted down the neck. He inspected the frets. Then he broke it over his knee."

Susan looked at her hands.

John said, "I don't want sympathy. You asked about symptoms. This is relevant. For years I thought of myself as 'John' while the Woodwards were calling me 'Benjamin.' After that day . . . for them, I *was*

Benjamin. I became what they wanted. Normal, adequate, pliant, and wholly unimpressive. You understand, it was an act. They noticed it, this change, but they never questioned it. They didn't want to. They welcomed it. I worked my body the way a puppeteer works a marionette. I *made up* Benjamin. He was my invention. In a way, he was as meticulous a piece of work as that guitar. I made him out of people I knew, out of what the Woodwards seemed to want. He was their natural child—maybe the child they deserved. I played Benjamin for almost three years, one thousand and eighty-five days. And when I turned sixteen I took my birth certificate and a hundred-dollar bill James Woodward kept in his sock drawer, and I left. Didn't look back, didn't leave a forwarding address . . . and I dropped Benjamin like a stone." He took a sip of cappucino. "At least I thought I did."

"What are you saying—that *Benjamin* was a symptom?"

"He *is* a symptom. He came back."

The Divide is a poignant tale of love and loss, of real people caught in frightening circumstances. It is a prime example of the evocative writing we have come to expect from Robert Charles Wilson—and an experience of the heart. Find out for yourself, when *The Divide* goes on sale in December 1989 wherever Doubleday Foundation trade paperbacks and hardcovers are sold.

ABOUT THE AUTHOR

ROBERT CHARLES WILSON was born in Whittier, California, in 1953, but has lived in Canada since the age of nine. He has worked at a number of jobs, including as a film extra and most recently with the Ontario Human Rights Commission. In addition to *A Hidden Place*, he is the author of three other highly acclaimed novels: *Memory Wire*, *Gypsies*, and *The Divide*. His short fiction has appeared in *The Magazine of Fantasy and Science Fiction* and *Isaac Asimov's Science Fiction Magazine*.